Boyfriends of Christmas Past

Boyfriends of Christmas Past

Edie Grace

TULE
PUBLISHING

Dear Reader,

It's almost Christmas! And nothing says holidays like creamy eggnog lattes, festive Christmas carols, and long, late nights at the office trying to secure your firm's most prized account…

Well, that is, if you're Emma Wallace.

We're all familiar with Dickens's *A Christmas Carol* and its infamous protagonist. But what if, instead of a bitter, miserly banker, Scrooge was an ambitious thirty-two-year-old career woman whose devoted boyfriend was growing tired of being stood up for endless hours at work? I'd had the idea for my gender-bending take on Dickens's classic for several years, but it wasn't until I decided to have the truth-telling "ghosts" be our heroine's ex-boyfriends that I knew I had a story worth sharing—and then I couldn't get it down fast enough! Now our dear Emma is about to get a wake-up call from not one but *four* exes who are very determined to help her see the error of her ways before this Christmas finds her alone under the mistletoe…

So…without further ado, I present to you my version of Christmas's famous cautionary tale, with the fervent and festive hope that you have as much fun reading *Boyfriends of Christmas Past* as I had writing it.

(Oh—and if you should find yourself craving Christmas cookies along the way, never fear: I've supplied you with a recipe at the story's end!)

Happy Holidays!!

XXOO,
Edie

Chapter One

E MMA WAS GOING to be late—there was no question about it. And even worse, long before she'd glanced up from her cluttered desk at five fifteen and felt the prickles of panic shoot across her scalp, she'd known of her inevitable truancy.

Because, truthfully, Emma Wallace had known she'd be delayed meeting her boyfriend, Sam Cole, for dinner at their favorite restaurant the minute she'd walked into her office at Zenith Media that morning and learned that the Johnson Cookware account was up for grabs again—and her proposal was getting a second shot.

So why hadn't she texted to let Sam know way back then?

That was, of course, the question Emma tried to ignore as her stylus flew wildly over page after page, reworking her initial ideas for the cookware company's new look—her gaze zooming from paper to computer screen with equal speed as she madly worked—telling herself her boyfriend would surely understand that after ten years in digital design, Emma was, at thirty-two, finally due the break of her career.

"Still here?" Vanessa appeared in Emma's doorway, her colleague's cloud of strawberry blonde curls bursting out of the bottom of a purple beret. After being cubicle neighbors at Zenith for four years, the fellow designer was more than just a trusted coworker. She was Emma's best friend. "So how's the redesign going?"

"I wish I knew," Emma said, reaching back to make a twist of her hair and snapping an elastic around the tidy knot. "One minute I think Diane's going to love it, the next minute I think a first-grader could come up with a better concept."

Vanessa leaned into the jamb. "Sounds like you could use a little something to sweeten your mood right now too. Want to grab an eggnog latte with me at Cocoa's?" The café's seasonal special was their favorite elixir for work stress—any other night Emma would have accepted the invitation.

"I wish I could, but I don't dare stop while the ideas are flowing."

"No worries—I understand."

But Emma swore a flicker of disappointment crossed her best friend's face before she looked away. What did Vanessa mean by, "Sounds like you could use a little something to sweeten your mood right now *too*?" Her friend was still feeling the aches and pains of a recent breakup—had today been especially tough? Emma would have gladly offered counsel, but buried this deep under deadline, she could only offer a warm smile—and an apology. "I'm really sorry, Ness. At this rate, I'm not even sure I'll make it to dinner with Sam."

Vanessa's thoughtful expression turned fierce. "Don't you dare cancel," she said, fixing Emma with a hard look. "Do you know how lucky he was to get a reservation at Ivy's this close to Christmas?"

She knew, all right. And the creeping remorse wasn't exactly helping her creative flow. Then again, neither was the relentless chime of Christmas carols their receptionist Denise insisted on playing on her computer.

Fortunately, Sam would understand her late arrival. After three years together, her boyfriend had grown accustomed to Emma's devotion to her work. After all, he had a demanding job too—although she would be hard-pressed to recall one time her architect boyfriend had ever been late for one of their dates—a record that, she'd admit, often stirred more than a few tremors of guilt. Tonight, however, she worked to tamp them down before they could start.

"Just don't push it too late," Vanessa said, turning to go. "As far as I know, Uber hasn't started offering teleportation service yet."

"If only." Emma grinned. "Oh, and do me a favor, will you? When you pass reception, can you ask Denise to turn down her music?"

"I most certainly will not. *Some* of us actually like getting into the holiday spirit. You know, holiday? As in, taking a break?"

"Denise started playing Christmas songs in *October*—you'll forgive me if my holiday spirit doesn't have a three-month shelf life," Emma said, spinning back to face her desk. "Besides—deadlines don't take holidays."

"Careful now, my friend…" Vanessa raised one side of her mouth in a smirk. "You're starting to sound like another person I know who always put work before fun."

"Oh yeah, who's that?"

"Ebenezer Scrooge."

EMMA PUSHED THROUGH Ivy's double doors at six forty-two and scanned the crowded restaurant with her heart in her throat for several seconds before she spotted Sam at a booth in the back, his brown hair falling over his forehead in the sexy, just-woke-up way that had sent butterflies of heat fluttering through her stomach the first time they'd met. Three years in, it still did. Only tonight, those butterflies were competing with the batting wings of nerves as she hurried across the busy floor.

Despite the lack of Christmas music in favor of a live bluegrass duo, there was no confusion as to the season. Twinkle lights swung from the exposed beams and wrapped around the room's unfinished wood columns, and every table boasted a festive centerpiece of pine boughs and holly sprigs, the thick, sappy scent of fresh pine nearly overpowering the smell of sautéed garlic.

"Baby, I am so, so sorry," Emma blurted breathlessly as she slid into the bench.

"Me too." Sam's voice was uncharacteristically tight, sending a knot of regret sinking in her stomach. His gaze remained fixed on his menu. "The couple over there just got the last order of scallops."

"I know you're angry."

"Believe it or not, I'm actually impressed. I'd bet you'd be an hour late, and here you are, just under fifty minutes." The strained smile he offered as she shrugged out of her coat did little to mask his sarcasm.

Then Emma saw the ramekin of crème brûlée in front of her and she sucked in an appreciative breath.

Sam gave a shrug. "I overheard the waiter say they were running low on those too."

She looked up at him, flushed with affection as she scanned his warm eyes. "I don't deserve you, do I?"

"Nope," he said flatly, and with just the right amount of gravity that Emma waited a beat before smiling, not sure if he was kidding or not.

Their waiter arrived to take their orders. Suddenly starving, she chose the broiled salmon with quinoa and an extra side of the restaurant's famous curry fries.

Sam gave her a wary look as he handed the waiter back their menus. "Let me guess—you skipped lunch again?"

"I ate a protein bar," she said, though, *inhaled* might have been a better verb. But who had time to waste eating? "I had a good reason," she said, leaning forward, bursting. "I have amazing news. Diane announced that Simon's presentation to Johnson Cookware was a total flop."

He stared at her, one sandy blond eyebrow arching dubiously. "I'm waiting for the part where you tell me the amazing news."

"It's amazing because Johnson said they'd be willing to look at the other proposals before going to another firm—which means I can finally get my ideas in front of Diane and knock their socks off!"

Sam reached for his water. "Don't you mean their aprons?"

Emma smiled, her racing nerves finally calming. Though there was no denying she'd been dazzled by Sam's bright blue eyes when she'd first met him, his sense of humor was, without a doubt, his very best feature.

"I've got some news too…" He opened his napkin and laid it across his lap. "We got the additional grant to keep Kids Who Cook going another year."

"*Sam!*" She clapped a hand over her forehead, feeling the flush of remorse burning there, remembering he was supposed to hear the news today. "Baby, I'm so sorry—I totally forgot to ask. That's fantastic! We should be toasting you." She reached for her wine then stopped. "Wait—we should order champagne!"

"It's a grant for ten thousand dollars, Em—not ten million," Sam said dryly, raising his glass. "Wine'll do."

"Still! It's amazing news." She tapped her wine to his, meeting his tender gaze over the rim as she took a sip. "I really *am* sorry, Sam," she said, setting her glass back down. "And not just because I forgot to ask about the grant."

Finally, a smile melted across his face, thawing the last of the chill he'd been wearing since she'd sat down. "Baby, it's okay. I know how disappointed you were not to get a shot at this account the first time around. And if a few late arrivals is what I have to trade so we can leave Saturday morning for my folks' house, then I'll gladly white-knuckle it."

Heat flooded her face. She blinked up at him, her voice nearly cracking as she asked, "Christmas is *this* Saturday?"

"Yup." Sam grinned. "I sent the big guy a text asking for an extension for you this year, but he turned me down. Sorry, babe."

A chuckle was the appropriate response, but Emma didn't dare risk choking on the knot of panic in her throat. Instead, she reached for her glass again and took a longer swig this time, hoping to force the ball of nerves down, but it remained lodged in her throat. When Diane had notified the design team this morning that they had until December twenty-third to polish their original campaigns for resubmission, Emma hadn't realized that date was only days away.

After three years of dating—and declining the invitation to spend Christmas with Sam's parents for every one of

7

them—she had known she couldn't say no a fourth year in a row. But she'd made that promise two months ago, before she'd gotten the second chance to win her dream account.

"*Em…*"

When she looked up, she found Sam's eyes trained on hers and pooling with dread.

"We are still on for this, right?"

"Of course!" The waiter returned with their order of bruschetta, his timing the perfect rescue, allowing Emma a few extra minutes to continue tamping down her rising nerves as she and Sam each dug into a slice.

"Speaking of my folks," he said. "My mom keeps forgetting about the whole pescatarian thing—even though I've told her you only eat fish no less than two hundred times."

Emma smiled as she unfolded her napkin. "At least your mother knows it's a dietary choice. When I explained it to my mom, she thought it meant I was going to a new church."

"Pescatarian, Episcopalian…" Sam grinned. "It's an easy mistake."

"It's okay, really. I don't want her making a special dish just for me."

"Are you kidding?" he snorted. "Elaine isn't *making* anything. She's ordering in the whole spread from her favorite restaurant."

Of course, Sam's mother wasn't cooking a single dish herself.

Unlike most people, whose passion for cooking came from watching their parents make meals, Sam's fondness came from the opposite. While most of his male friends could barely boil water if someone else didn't fill the pot for them, Sam was an accomplished and entirely self-taught chef, a passion he'd detailed to Emma on their first date. Growing up the oldest of three boys, Sam had been responsible for making his younger brothers' meals when his parents had been gone at all hours to run the family's insurance business. And though his brothers had soon developed their own erratic schedules, thanks to sports practices and other after-school commitments, and had no longer needed him to cook for them, Sam's passion for cooking hadn't dimmed. When the local elementary school had wanted to offer after-school programs, he had volunteered to teach cooking lessons. Two years later, he'd turned a few classes for a handful of elementary students into a wildly popular neighborhood program called Kids Who Cook.

The news of his culinary expertise had excited Emma from the start—not just because she was a hopeless cook and looked forward to enjoying his skills, but because she also liked knowing he had grown up living with people who'd made sacrifices for their careers, so her own demanding and often unpredictable work schedule wouldn't be hard for him to adjust to. And in their three years together, it hadn't been.

At least, not that she had ever witnessed.

"So you think you'll have a better shot the second time around?"

He was steering them back to talk of her work—a good sign the sting of her late arrival had finally softened.

She smiled gratefully. "I'm hoping."

"Have you told your folks yet?"

"So my mom can tell me I work too hard and that I should be working toward settling down instead?" Emma shook her head. "No thanks."

Her mother, a nurse with a great-paying job when she'd married Emma's father, had chosen to stay home after Emma was born—a decision Emma always believed she must have regretted, living with her penny-pinching father. Having grown up watching her mother be put through the ringer just to buy light bulbs, Emma vowed from an early age to make her own money—money she could spend however she wanted and didn't have to ask permission for from anyone.

Sam chuckled as he reached for his glass.

"What's so funny?" she asked.

"It just occurred to me…" He swirled his wine.

"What did?"

His eyes appraised her tenderly, all traces of the earlier frost gone. "The cosmic irony in a woman who can't cook landing a major cookware account."

Chapter Two

THEY EXITED THE restaurant at nine to find a fine layer of flurries had dusted downtown while they'd eaten. Just enough flakes to make for a glittering winter wonderland but not require shoveling, and definitely not enough to make the sidewalks treacherous. Still, Emma took the opportunity to thread her arm through Sam's as he walked her back the few blocks to her condo where he'd parked.

"So I guess this deadline means I'll have to take a rain check for tomorrow night's dinner, huh?" he asked, clapping one of his gloved hands over hers where it curved in the warm crook of his arm.

Emma sighed. "I'm afraid so," she said, laying her cheek on his sleeve. Even through the thick down, she could detect the familiar woodsy spice of his soap underneath, sending her pulse racing.

They reached the front of her townhouse, the pine wreath on the door—a gift from the condo association— bearing the fresh glitter of the night's flurries.

Sam scanned the decoration, his gaze hanging on the pair of *papier-mâché* turtle doves nestled at the base of the fir circle. "As festive as this is," he said, "you think you could ask the association to spring for a cluster of mistletoe next year instead?"

"I'll bring it up at the next meeting."

Sam stepped close and pulled her into his arms. "Tell you what—I'll make the fish curry anyway and just drop it off. I won't stay. I won't even come in. I'll just hand it to you through the door."

"*Through the door?*" She tilted her head and gave him a dubious squint. Neither of them had that kind of willpower in one another's company.

Even now, the cold having turned the tip of her nose a shade of red even Rudolph would envy, it was going to be a struggle to untangle herself from his arms when all she wanted was to invite him inside to stretch out their night in front of a roaring fire. They could curl up on the couch, watch the flames grow tall, and warm each other up…

Her breathing hastened just thinking about it. She'd have to be strong for both of them. "If you really don't want to distract me from finishing this presentation, baby, don't come by tomorrow night…" Emma smiled. "With *or* without dinner."

Sam's brow, and voice, lowered sternly. "You have to eat."

"So you keep reminding me."

"Not to mention, it's bad karma to starve yourself while working on a campaign for cookware."

She laughed. "Just like it's bad karma to keep someone's calzone order, right?" she asked with a wry smile, referring to the switched takeout bags that had brought them together three years earlier on an equally crisp winter night.

"At least promise you'll swing by the school on your way home tomorrow," Sam said. "A few of us are coming in to make extra cookies for Friday night's packing party."

Emma dipped her chin, hoping to hide the worried flush that threatened to flood her cheeks. In her enthusiastic haze to redo the Johnson presentation, Christmas wasn't the only event she'd let slip from her memory. Tomorrow night's gathering at the school to assemble the Christmas cookie care packages—complete with personal, handmade Christmas cards from the students to deliver to Sunshine Village Retirement Home on Christmas Eve day—was a very big deal, both to the community and to Sam and the rest of the volunteers. Just like holiday meals at his parents' house, Emma had too often found herself having to miss events for Sam's Kids Who Cook program for work commitments.

And just like Christmas dinner, she had made a vow this year to attend the after-school program's annual celebration—no matter what.

"I'll swing by. But you've got to promise me, Sam. No surprise visits tomorrow night." She unlocked her door and glanced up at him. "I'd ask you in, but—"

"I know, I know. White-knuckling it." He reached down and cupped her face; Emma pressed her cheek against his hand. "Just promise me you'll actually get some sleep at some point tonight, okay?"

Clearly he'd forgotten that, unlike him, she hadn't ordered decaf with dessert. "I make no promises."

"Fair enough." He dropped a warm, heavy kiss on her lips. Emma could still taste the nutmeg from the eggnog ice cream he'd ordered with his coffee. Three years after their first kiss, and her heart still fluttered when he dipped his face toward hers, anticipation flickering through her ribs.

When their second kiss deepened, she pressed her hands begrudgingly against his chest to stop them.

Sam stepped back, his gloved hands raised. "This is me going," he said as he walked backward down the snow-dusted walkway.

"Goodnight, Going," she teased, waving him off.

Even after he'd disappeared around the corner, Emma could still feel the heat of his embrace warming her skin. Turning back to her door, she let her wistful gaze drift over the wreath as she inserted her key and turned the knob. It really was a pretty wreath. She especially liked the beads of holly threaded through the boughs, and the tiny doves *were* a lovely touch, their shimmering silver wings, and their warm little black eyes—

Emma's hand froze mid-twist.

Was she dreaming, or had one of the birds just *winked* at her?

She blinked hard, staring between the two birds, but the

only movement was the brushing of the breeze along the tips of the pine needles, sending sequins of snow flurries shimmering through the air.

Just the wind. She shook her head at herself for being so foolish as the lock gave and she pushed her door open.

Inside, she flung off her coat and hat and dashed for her desk in the corner of her bedroom, doing the math in her head even as she tapped her laptop on and stared at the screen, waiting for it to blink to life.

Forty-eight hours.

She had forty-eight hours between now and Friday night to rework her designs into the presentation of her career. And, okay, if she needed a few extra hours Saturday morning, she and Sam could always blame it on traffic—

No.

Emma rolled back her shoulders, chastising herself. She wouldn't have to make excuses. She could do this. After all, she already had most of her ideas sketched out—it was just a matter of adjusting them to reflect Johnson's critique of Simon's ideas, right? And, of course, getting Diane to love them as much as Emma knew her boss would. Because Emma didn't kid herself that there would be plenty of junior designers who would gladly forsake yule logs and stocking stuffing to produce a killer rebranding campaign.

Two hours later, she'd reworked a third of her sketches. A good beginning, but only a start. Her screen blinked the time. 12:46. Her eyes felt heavy. So much for that espresso with dessert.

Emma glanced over at her bed, the duvet looking especially cloud-like, the pillows particularly puffy and soft. She'd just put her head down for a sec, she decided as she untied the knot of her hair and fell, still dressed, on top of her made bed, confident that if she didn't get under the covers, she wouldn't sleep more than a few minutes. And that was all she needed, really.

Just a little catnap to refresh, and then she'd get right back to it…

Chapter Three

E MMA HEARD HER name.

At least, she thought she did. But when she opened her eyes and looked around her bedroom, she was alone. Of course she would be; she'd obviously just been dreaming. She lunged for the clock on her nightstand and spun it around. 4:45 a.m. An exasperated breath escaped her. She hadn't meant to sleep so long.

Stumbling to her feet, she hurried into the bathroom, sure a splash of cold water would wake her up, and cupped her hands under the rushing tap.

"*Emma!*"

Her face tipped down, she froze, blinking through the droplets of water that still clung to her eyelashes.

"*Emma Wallace!*"

She wasn't dreaming anymore. Someone had called her name. A *male* someone.

A male someone *in her house.*

Her heart thumping, she darted for the door, slammed it shut, and locked it—only to realize her folly in the next second when she looked around at her windowless bathroom. How was she supposed to get out?

She reached for the medicine cabinet to ransack it for possible weapons when the voice rang out again.

"Emma, it's me—Scott Fields!"

Scott Fields?

She looked over at the closed door, the familiar name floating through her thoughts, looking for anchor...

Wait. Her high school boyfriend's name was Scott Fields. Scott Fields was in her house?

Emma tiptoed toward the door and pressed her ear to the wood, straining to hear movement on the other side, but all she could hear was the rushing of her pulse in her ears.

No. There was another noise. Was it...bouncing?

A few more seconds of listening and she was certain. Someone was bouncing a ball in her bedroom.

Correction. Scott Fields, her high school boyfriend, was bouncing a ball in her bedroom.

She glanced over at her reflection, seeing her still-damp face staring back at her, her hazel eyes huge, her blond hair as frazzled as her expression. She reached up, plucked out a stray strand, and winced. If she was dreaming, she wouldn't have felt that, right?

Either way, she couldn't spend the rest of this night in her bathroom. She had work to finish—and if Christmas wasn't going to stop her, then no way was the hallucination of her ex-boyfriend's bouncing basketball going to either. There had to be a rational explanation for all this—and she would find it.

Newly fortified, Emma pulled in a steeling breath, opened the door, and stepped carefully back into the inky blue-black of her bedroom.

"There you are! I wondered how long you planned on hanging out in there."

Hearing the voice, she rushed to the wall and threw on the overhead, flooding the room with light. Blinking against the glare, she squinted as she scanned the space, but her bedroom was empty.

"I'm over here, Emma. On your computer."

Ice water filled her veins.

Slowly, she turned to her desk. Sure enough, there on the screen of her laptop, in his basketball uniform, his dark hair coiled with sweat, dribbling a ball with one hand and waving to her with the other, was Scott Fields.

If Emma's legs were still keeping her up, it had to have been by magic, because she couldn't feel them. Then again, she couldn't feel her fingers either. "This is a dream, I'm dreaming," she murmured dully. "Everyone knows you get crazy dreams when you eat ice cream right before bed."

"That's actually a myth," Scott said with the same authoritarian tone he'd always used to answer questions in Mr. Roth's chemistry class. "There's no actual scientific proof that food correlates to dream activity. I know because I did my senior science fair project on that very subject. You of all people should remember—you helped me make that giant *papier-mâché* ice cream cone."

Emma swallowed. Was she having a stroke? It was possible. She'd heard of people younger than herself suffering from undiagnosed heart problems. What about a fever? She clapped a hand over her forehead. Was she burning up?

"You're not having a heart attack, Emma," Scott said, still dribbling. "Look, I know this is all weird, but bear with me, okay?" More voices rang out—Scott looked to his left as if there might be something, or some*one*, in the wings of all that white, and shouted, "Be right there, guys!" He turned back to her. "Hey, I gotta make this quick—Chuck and Keith want to go shoot some hoops before the game." He stilled the basketball and cradled it against his chest. "Okay, so here's the deal—you need some serious help. And I don't mean, like, homework help, I mean, like, *life* help. Because between you and me, you're about to screw up. *Big time.*"

She blinked at the screen.

"Listen," Scott continued, "I don't know what happened after us, but apparently you've been blowing it with boy-friends for a while now—"

"Excuse me?"

He shrugged. "Hey, I'm just telling you what they told me—"

"*They?*"

"And since it looks like you're heading for breakup-ville again with this Sam guy, it's time to bring in the big guns before you lose him. I'd love to be the guy to walk you through this, but I just turned eighteen and I still have to pass my driver's test, so they got someone else to do it. Actually, *three* someones. Three boyfriends, more specifically." Scott leaned forward and snickered. "So much for telling me you'd never love another guy as long as you lived after we broke up, huh? *Busted.*"

Emma flinched. Was she honestly getting guilt-tripped by an ice cream dream?

Wait. Had he said she'd be visited by three old boyfriends? Just like Scrooge was visited by three ghosts in *A Christmas Carol*—and hadn't Vanessa compared her to Ebenezer Scrooge earlier tonight? No wonder she was having this dream! "So you're telling me I'm going to be visited by three ghosts?"

"Not ghosts—old boyfriends."

Which, she might have argued, weren't necessarily different things—but before she could, a clatter came from the kitchen.

She spun to her bedroom doorway, the doughy smell of hot pizza suddenly filling the room. She'd had vivid dreams before, but she couldn't recall any being *scented*.

Scott smiled. "Sounds like ex-boyfriend number one just arrived."

Chapter Four

"**Y**O, EMMALOU! WHAT'S *shakin'?*"

Emma walked out of her bedroom and sucked in a sharp breath. "Oh, my God…" She squinted. "Michael?"

She whispered his name like a question, but there was no doubt that the man leaning against her kitchen counter with a half-eaten slice of pizza hanging from his hand was her college boyfriend, Michael Rogers. And he looked exactly as he had the first time she'd ever laid eyes on him in the student union, his blond hair shaggy, wearing a ratty Kappa Sigma Omega T-shirt, faded jeans, and flip-flops.

The streak of spilled pizza sauce across the hem, however, was new.

"Michael, what—what are you doing here?" Emma might have added *in my kitchen* and *looking as if you've never seen the passage of time*, but a more general inquiry seemed best.

"Jeez, and you chicks say us guys never listen?" Michael snorted. "*Hellooo?* The dude on the computer just told you all this, Emmalou, remember? A few of us would be swinging by, checking in to help you… Any of this ringing a bell?" he

22

asked, waving his wedge of pizza in the air for emphasis. "Man, I hope you took better notes in class."

Emma narrowed her eyes hotly. Oh, this was rich. Getting lectured on good study habits by the guy who skipped his anatomy final to see the first showing of the new *Star Wars* movie. What had she ever seen in Michael, anyway? Sure, he was fun, always up for a road trip or a party, but eventually a person had to grow up and get serious.

And was he honestly still calling her by that ridiculous nickname?

"Hungry?" Michael pushed the pizza box toward her. "Take a slice for the road." She blinked at the name on the side—Bruno's. Wow. Not only was her college boyfriend standing in her kitchen, but he'd somehow managed to get a pizza from their favorite college restaurant delivered. As dreams went, this one definitely deserved points for detail.

She glanced down at the pie, the sea of cheese and mushrooms glistening with pools of grease, and her stomach rolled.

She grimaced. "No thanks."

"Right, I forgot—you always liked it better cold." Pushing the last piece of crust into his mouth, Michael wiped his hands clean on his seat then freed another slice for himself.

Had he said take a slice for the road?

Emma almost didn't dare ask. "Are we going somewhere?"

"Out."

"Let me guess. You have some magic car, right?"

"Emmalou." Michael gave her a disparaging look. "I just pulled an all-nighter watching *The Matrix* trilogy. I'm not getting behind any wheel of any car—magic or not."

Funny, she didn't recall him being so responsible in college.

He bit off the point of his fresh slice and hitched his chin toward the front door as he chewed, explaining after he'd swallowed. "We'll be walking."

"Then I'll go get my coat." If she could smell mushroom pizza in this dream, then she'd *definitely* feel below-freezing air.

But Michael put up a hand to stop her. "Don't bother," he said, giving the knob a twist and swinging the front door wide open. "You won't need one where we're going."

❧

AS SOON AS Emma followed him over the threshold, she stopped.

Hours earlier, the exterior of her apartment building had been on the other side of this door. But now, stepping through, Emma found herself not outside but still inside, only the room she had walked into wasn't any she'd been in recently. In fact, based on the wall calendar that hung above one of the room's two particle-board desks, she hadn't been in it since 2009. And with good reason—that was the year she'd graduated college.

As impossible as it was to believe, she was standing in the middle of her dorm room.

And there, in front of their shared wall mirror, was her college roommate Mindy, twisting to check out all angles of her shimmering black velvet dress.

Another burst of confusion rushed over her—again she recalled Scott Fields's instructions and forced her quizzical mind to quiet. *Just go with it, Emma. You can do that for once, can't you?* After all, she'd had plenty of stress-induced dreams in her life—at least this one might prove entertaining. Michael might have been lazy as a student, but when it came to searching out the best time on campus, no one worked harder.

Emma glanced around the cramped room, a thought sparking. "Shouldn't I be here too?" she whispered.

"You'll be here in a second," Michael said around another bite of pizza. "You're coming back from the computer lab. And you don't have to whisper, by the way. She can't hear or see us."

The faint pulse of dance music thumped from somewhere in the building. "Where's that music coming from?"

"The holiday party in the common room. It's rocking. Hard. They've already spiked the eggnog."

She frowned. "I don't remember going."

"That's because you didn't. We had plans to meet up at Beanie's Café and then go together. But you stood me up to chase down your professor instead."

Emma bristled, recalling the night in question now. Professor Donatelli, whose mixed-media seminar was the most sought-after class in the entire department. "I didn't *chase him down*," she said tightly. "I had a meeting with him."

"Call it what you want. All I know is you drove out to his house before he left for Christmas break to beg him to give you a spot in some seminar."

"Well, it was worth it," she said proudly. "He let me in the class."

"I'm glad to hear that—because it caused us to break up."

Emma frowned, mining her memories. She remembered when she'd stopped seeing Michael—it had been winter, because she recalled him coming back to her room a few days later to pick up his ski gloves—but she hadn't remembered the specific scene. Only that neither one of them had been too terribly broken up over it.

"Watch," Michael said, nodding toward the door. "You'll see."

In the next instant, the door opened, and Emma sucked in a startled breath to see her twenty-year-old self blow in, arms loaded with books, which she dumped on her unmade bed with a loud sigh. Her outfit now revealed, Emma winced at the familiar polka-dotted print. "God, I remember that horrible sweater."

"Hey," Michael said with a playful pout. "I loved that

sweater. You looked hot in it."

She smiled, feeling the faint flush of his compliment. Who knew she could blush in her dreams?

Mindy paused to apply her lipstick. "Are you okay? You look stressed out."

"I just found out Donatelli is adding two more spots in the mixed media seminar and I *totally* have to have one," Emma's old self said breathlessly.

If it had been a shock to see her old self, hearing herself was an equal shock. Especially since she'd conveniently forgotten her fondness for including the word *totally* in every sentence—a habit she'd broken eventually, thank goodness.

"So ask him to let you in the class when we get back from break," Mindy said, giving her makeup a final inspection.

"I can't wait until then, Min—I totally have to ask him now. Tonight."

Emma's roommate shot her a dubious look as she crossed to her dresser. "But you're going out with Michael tonight. And, besides, it's Christmas break. All the faculty are gone."

"Just because they're off campus doesn't mean they're gone, right?" Emma's double pointed out with a mischievous grin.

Passing the mirror again, Mindy slowed. "I'm still not sure whether to go heels or boots," she said, pointing to her black pumps. "What do you think?"

"I think he's going to give the spots to seniors."

Mindy's dark eyes narrowed with exasperation. "I meant about the shoes, Em."

"Oh. Sorry."

But Emma was hard pressed to find evidence of apology in her old self's distracted gaze.

Michael shook his head condemningly. "Man, self-absorbed much?"

"I was stressed out," Emma defended, even as her throat tightened with remorse. "Mindy was my friend—she under-stood how serious I was about my degree."

"Sounds like you expect lots of *understanding* from the people in your life."

She glared up at him. What was *that* supposed to mean?

Okay, fine. Maybe she had been flaky in college, but she knew how to be a good friend now…didn't she?

Her earlier exchange with Vanessa crept back, her friend's request to grab a latte and her poorly veiled disap-pointment when Emma had declined. Clearly, Vanessa had needed a friend to talk to tonight. Even if Emma couldn't have spared the half hour for a trip down the block to Cocoa's, she could've at least stopped working for five minutes to offer counsel…

A knock sounded.

"That'll be me," Michael said to Emma, leaning over.

Sure enough, Mindy opened the door to reveal Michael on the other side.

Her college roommate stepped back to let him enter.

"Since I can't seem to get an answer out of your girlfriend, I'll ask you—pumps or boots?"

He grinned. "Can I vote for bare feet?"

"Heels it is." Mindy rolled her eyes as she skirted around him for the door. "Have fun, kids."

"What happens now?" Emma whispered, just in case Michael was wrong about the not-hearing-them part.

"Sorry, can't tell you. Gotta let you see for yourself. Those are the rules."

Since when did dreams have rules? "Oh, goody," Emma muttered sourly, shifting on her heels as she watched herself and Michael's double come together in the middle of the room. Making things even weirder was the fact that, while the Emma she observed looked distinctly younger than herself, Michael's dream figure looked the same age as the guy who had been taking her on this strange trip—even down to the same faded jeans.

But when she watched Michael sweep her younger self up into a deep kiss, Emma's cheeks warmed.

She glanced over to find Michael grinning proudly as he watched the scene. "Bet you forgot what an awesome kisser I was, huh?"

Emma tried to bite back a confirming smile but couldn't. He *had* been a great kisser.

She, however, looked like a fish singing opera! Was that honestly the face she made when she was kissing someone? No wonder people always kept their eyes closed!

She leaned over. "I thought you said this was the night we broke up?"

"Not here," said Michael. "Later. In a second, you're going to tell me you just remembered you promised someone you'd give them a lift to the bus station tonight, so you might be a little late meeting me at Beanie's."

In other words, she was going to lie to him. Even in dream, Emma felt tremors of remorse flutter through her stomach. But just as she opened her mouth to ask when, the room, so clear seconds earlier, began to blur, smearing into a colorful but indistinct haze. Emma squinted, trying to make out shapes as the shifting mist settled again, this time revealing a different space. Beanie's. The campus coffee house was bright and crowded and festive with holiday decorations. The sweet smell of freshly baked eggnog scones floated in the air. A jazzy instrumental version of "Winter Wonderland" piped through the speakers, loud enough to be heard above the clatter of dishes and conversations. The three baristas who hurried behind the counter all wore goofy Santa hats. Emma remembered feeling bad for them even then.

"You're sure they can't see us?" she whispered, looking out into the packed room.

"Positive. Watch—I'll prove it," Michael said, then proceeded to leap up onto the nearest empty chair, puff out his chest, and grace the room with several loud, and painfully off-key, bars from "Jingle Bells"—a demonstration that made

Emma cringe but, to her immeasurable relief, had absolutely no effect on anyone else in the entire coffee shop.

Done, Michael jumped down with a satisfied smile. "Told you."

Emma rolled her eyes. God, he was such a goofball. "So are *we* here somewhere?" she asked, craning her neck to search through the curtain of caffeinated coeds for herself and Michael.

"*We* aren't," said Michael. "But I am."

Emma followed his index finger to the back of the café, where she spotted Michael slouched at a small round table, his expression uncharacteristically grim. He held his mouth in a hard line. His brow, usually in a perpetual state of playful wiggling, was knitted tightly. "You look mad."

Michael nodded. "That's because I was."

"But I said I was going to be late," she defended hotly.

"You weren't late, Emmalou. You never showed."

Emma stepped back, the reminder like a shove. "I guess I forgot that part," she admitted quietly.

"That isn't the only thing you forgot." Michael pointed her attention back to his old self just in time for Emma to watch him pull out a small, rectangular jewelry box and snap it open, staring forlornly at whatever was inside. "In case you're wondering, it was a charm bracelet," he said, a noticeable edge of disappointment deepening in his usually chipper voice.

She looked over at him, stunned. "You bought me a

31

Christmas gift?"

"Not just Christmas. It was our one-year anniversary."

She shifted her gaze back to the scene, trying to absorb this news. No wonder he'd been so upset that she'd stood him up to find her professor. Another bolt of regret charged up the back of her neck, hotter this time. But she wasn't going to take *all* the blame. "Why didn't you tell me it was our anniversary?"

"Why did I have to?" Michael frowned at her. "Jeez, Emmalou. We were both in the relationship. You could have done the math too—if you'd cared enough. Obviously you didn't."

"You actually kept track?"

"Look, I'll admit I could be a slacker—a pretty big one most of the time—but I never slacked off on the things that were important to me. Or the people."

Emma lowered her gaze sheepishly. She'd always remembered Michael as a player, a guy who never wanted the commitment and responsibility of a girlfriend. "Michael, I'm—I'm sorry…"

But when she looked up again, he was gone. Then, the whole café was gone too. In its place was the milky haze of sunlight, pressing through her flickering eyelids, demanding entrance.

Chapter Five

8:50?

Seeing the time on her phone screen, Emma bolted from her bed and dashed into the bathroom, groaning as she groped for the shower knob and swinging it on full-blast. How did it get to be so late? Not only had she let a catnap turn into a full night's sleep, but she'd overslept to boot.

Too rushed to stop for coffee, she slugged down a can of Coke as she drove and thanked her stars that she'd ended up saving that oversized candy cane they'd passed out at the last staff meeting—it would be enough of a sugar rush to get her through to lunch.

Stopped at a light, snippets of her crazy dream flashed back at her. Scott on her computer. Michael offering her Bruno's pizza. The interior of the campus coffee house. The sweet, creamy smell of eggnog scones…

It had all seemed so *real.*

Rushing out of the elevator fifteen minutes later, she found Diane Jackson waiting for her in her cubicle, her boss's copper coils fanned out against the back of Emma's chair, her red-cowboy-booted feet propped up on Emma's desk, and her crimson-lacquered lips curled around a candy cane—the same one Emma had been counting on to be her emergency breakfast.

Diane pulled the striped candy out her mouth and held it up. "Did you know that ERs see hundreds of cases of candy cane-related injuries every Christmas?"

Emma managed a strained smile. Leave it to her boss to find a dark spot in the season of lights. "Um, no. I didn't know that."

Diane's pensive gaze shifted to her and narrowed. "Emma, how long have you been working here?"

Prickles of panic danced across her scalp. Was this some kind of impromptu performance evaluation? Because this really, *really* wasn't a good day. Emma proceeded with caution. "Five years."

"Do you know I went from designer to director in *three*?"

Of course Emma knew. Everyone who worked at Zenith knew. Because, much in the same way she could count on them to always bring out Santa at the end of every Macy's Thanksgiving Day parade, Diane could always be counted on to regale her staff with her own rise-through-the-ranks story at every office Christmas party. Emma, it seemed, was getting a preview of this year's event.

"Incredible," she said, forcing the higher register of awe to her voice.

"Emma, do you know why I hired you?" Technically, it had been the previous director who had hired her, but Emma wasn't about to nitpick. "Because when I asked every candidate where they saw themselves in ten years, you were the only one who didn't see herself with a family. And I thought to myself, *this* is someone who knows what she wants."

Two days ago, the reminder would have filled Emma with a fierce balloon of pride—today, however, she felt a strange pang of regret.

"Are you happy here, Emma?"

"Very." *No. Wait. This was a trick question.* She pursed her lips. "I mean, yes, I'm very happy *but…*"

Diane leaned forward expectantly. "But…"

"But I know I can do more. I *want* to do more here, Diane."

And just like that, her boss' glossy lips bloomed into a wide—albeit slightly Grinch-like—smile. Diane plucked the candy cane from her mouth with an audible pop and trained it on Emma like a laser pointer. "Jasper tells me you want to rework your designs for the Johnson rebranding."

"I do, yes."

"And you'll have something to show me before the holiday?"

"Absolutely. I'm nearly there."

"Excellent." Her boss lowered her feet and spun out of Emma's chair, tossing the barely touched candy cane into the trash as she waltzed past her.

Alone, Emma collapsed into her chair and leaned back, trying to calm her racing heart, but her pulse was still thundering when Vanessa swung in, no doubt having heard the tell-tale gunfire of Diane's cowboy boots clopping away down the corridor.

Vanessa carried a pair of coffees, one of which she set down in front of Emma.

"You're a *goddess*," Emma said, scooping up the cup and downing several sips.

"I'd settle for assistant goddess," Vanessa joked, taking the cubicle's other seat. She scanned Emma's face. "Are you okay? You look like you've seen a ghost."

"Two, actually," Emma muttered.

"Excuse me?"

Emma smiled as she set down her cup. "Nothing."

"So are you?" Vanessa whispered.

Now it was Emma's turn to look baffled. "Am I what?"

"Nearly there on your presentation?" her coworker asked then offered a sheepish shrug. "Hey, it isn't eavesdropping if you can't avoid hearing it."

"I will be. Between you and me, I didn't end up getting as much work done last night as I hoped."

"Let me guess…" Vanessa's lips spread into a suggestive smile behind the lid of her coffee. "Something—or some-*one*—take up your time instead?"

Emma offered a weak shrug in response, thinking it was the safest answer. How to explain to her good friend that the distraction had actually been sleep? Oh, and also the unexpected appearance of her college boyfriend leading her on a minute-by-minute tour of the night of their breakup. Even though images of the dream were fading from her memory, Emma still felt the sting of Michael's hurt vividly—and with it, shame.

"I take it you made it to the restaurant on time?" Vanessa asked.

"More or less," Emma lied, dipping her face into her cup for a quick sip before Vanessa could mine her gaze and see the unease she was sure pooled in them.

But when she looked up again, her friend's eyes remained intent—and dubious.

"I told you, Ness. Sam's not one of those men who feels threatened if I'm not making him the center of my universe twenty-four seven." Her thoughts shifted back to the dream again, and another flutter of regret—this one she *could* correct. "Hey, I'm sorry I wasn't there for you last night."

Vanessa waved her hand. "Don't worry about it. I know you were busy with this redesign."

"A friend should never be so busy that she can't grab an eggnog latte," Emma said. "Or give an opinion on a stupid pair of shoes."

"Shoes?" Vanessa blinked at her.

"Never mind." Emma smiled. "Just know if something's up and you want to talk, I'm here, okay?"

But Vanessa's gaze remained pointed. "Are you *sure* Sam didn't order you a side of crow to eat last night?"

"Very funny."

Still, her friend sat back in the chair and tented her laced fingers under her chin, training an exacting look on Emma. "It *has* occurred to you that he might pop the question while you're up at his folks' house, right?"

Emma stopped mid-sip and met Vanessa's leveled and expectant gaze over the top of her cup. The thought *had* crossed her mind, yes—and every time it did, Emma felt a dizzying charge of excitement—even as her head tried to overthrow her heart with reason.

"I doubt it. Sam and I have talked about this, and we both agree that things are too crazy in our careers right now to talk marriage. Besides, Sam would never propose around his parents. He knows his mother would plan some huge impromptu engagement party for us the very next day if we did it within fifty miles of their house, and you know how private he is."

Vanessa's dubious smirk remained. "All I know is that the mix of romance and Christmas is a heady cocktail, my friend, and it can make people—otherwise practical, *private* people—do crazy things."

Or dream them, apparently.

Vanessa leaned in, refusing to be ignored. "Admit it. Isn't there a tiny part of you that swoons at the thought of Sam making some grand gesture over the holiday?"

About as tiny as Texas, Emma wanted to say, but turned her attention to a pile of sketches, desperate for distraction, even as her heart hammered at the possibility. Despite having most of her waking moments in the past few weeks focused on coming up with a winning campaign for the Johnson account, she still found space to let the warm flickers of anticipation smolder too.

"I thought so," Vanessa said with a victorious snicker, clearly taking Emma's silence for confirmation of her theory. "Just promise you'll text me if he does."

She grinned. "And risk interrupting one of your father's traditional Christmas sing-alongs at the Forrester house?"

"Yes." Vanessa groaned. "*Especially* then."

Chapter Six

SINCE IT WAS after hours, Emma had to ring the bell at the front doors of Adams Elementary. A middle-aged woman with a blunt black bob told her to wait in the foyer while she went through a pair of double doors in search of Sam. Her boyfriend arrived a few minutes later, his navy tee heavily streaked with flour, more of it dusting the edges of his wavy brown hair, which he pointed to as he approached. "If you're thinking it's flour, it's not. Apparently twenty-five seven-year-olds have the power to turn a man prematurely gray."

She laughed, reaching up to brush some of the powder from his temples. "Are you sure you got enough flour in the actual cookies?"

"See for yourself," Sam said as he steered them down the hall toward the cafeteria kitchen. As they walked, Emma admired the student-made decorations that transformed the concrete-block walls into a winter wonderland—paper-cut snowflakes and snowmen, Christmas wreaths, and giant candy canes. The last time she'd visited Sam here—the *only* time, actually—she'd recalled displays of autumn leaves and pumpkins. Twice in two years was a pitiful record—which was all the more reason she was coming to the packing party tomorrow night, no matter what.

The clatter and high voices of excited children grew louder, signaling they were nearly there.

"So, how's the presentation coming along?" he asked.

"It's getting there. Diane seems excited that I want to resubmit my designs." Stopped in the opened doors of the cafeteria, Emma caught a warm, buttery whiff of just-baked sugar cookies. The festive scent filled her with a swell of celebration. "How's the cookie factory coming?"

"Let's just say if you lined up all the sugar cookies we made this afternoon, you'd end up at the North Pole."

She laughed. "All this talk of Christmas cookies and snow makes me want to burst out with 'Silver Bells.'"

"Wow." Sam pulled her against him and dropped a kiss on her nose. "Maybe there's hope for my little Scrooge yet."

Emma stiffened and reared back, startled.

"Whoa." Sam frowned down at her, as surprised by her response as she'd been at his comment. "Did I say something wrong?"

"No, it's just…" Feeling foolish, she softened and let her body fall against his again, burrowing deeper into his embrace. The heat of his body was like sinking into a warm bath. Her racing heart calmed instantly. "I had this crazy dream last night and I—"

"*Chef Sam! Chef Sam!*"

They turned to see a boy in a bulky green parka charging down the hall toward them, the backpack slung over his tiny shoulders nearly as big as he was. A pretty woman with the boy's same dark curls followed him, carrying a silver-and-gold striped gift bag.

"Hold that thought," Sam whispered as he released her and turned to greet their approaching company. When the little boy was closing in, Sam dropped down to his heels to be at eye level when he arrived. "So, how's everything in the kitchen, Eli?"

Coming to screeching halt, the little boy gave a woeful exhale and threw up his padded arms. "Terrible! Chloe won't stop eating the broken ones, and Ryan keeps trying to hide his dinosaur in the cookie dough!"

Emma rolled her lips together to keep from laughing—a technique she noticed the boy's mother employing too. Sam, however, didn't break character. He offered the boy a sympathetic nod, his brow bent with sufficient gravity. "Now you see why I left you in charge."

Eli raised his shoulders then let them fall with a deep sigh. "They're wearing me out."

Now Sam laughed.

Emma watched the exchange, swells of affection warming behind her ribs. Sam was so good with kids. He'd make a great dad, she had no doubt. So why did she feel the prickle of panic every time she thought about what kind of mom *she'd* make?

Sam climbed back to his feet to make the introductions between Emma and Eli's mother, Gail.

"It's nice to finally meet you," Gail said. "Sam's always talking about the famous Emma."

He was? Ripples of pride thrummed through her.

Sam smiled. "Guilty as charged."

"I hope you're coming to the packing party tomorrow night?" Gail asked.

She nodded. "I wouldn't miss it for the world."

"Good." The boy's mother raised the gift bag she carried, tufts of green and red tissue sprouting out of the top, and held it out to Sam. "Just a little something from a few of us moms to thank you for all you do for the kids," she said, her cheeks bearing a noticeable flush as Sam's face broke into an appreciative smile.

Emma had to believe most of the mothers had little crushes on Sam. She didn't blame them.

"Thanks so much," he said. "See you both tomorrow night."

"Absolutely," Gail said, taking Eli's hand to steer him toward the exit.

"Bye, Chef Sam!" The little boy charged off, still waving.

Alone again, Sam turned back to Emma, the comforting smile he'd flashed at Eli and his mother fading as he studied her face expectantly. "So, what happened?"

She looked up at him, searching his blue eyes for explanation.

"In your dream."

"Oh. That. It was just crazy."

"You said that already. What was so crazy about it?"

"I was back in college. In my old dorm room, and this guy Michael was there…"

Sam squinted. "Michael was your serious college boyfriend, right?"

She had never considered Michael particularly serious about *anything*, let alone their relationship, but after last night's dream, and how he'd confessed to her that—

No. Emma shook her head, shoving the ridiculous thought out of her mind like brushing crumbs off a placemat. What was wrong with her? Michael hadn't confessed anything—Michael hadn't even been there!

You had a dream, Emma. Michael was no more there than Scott was waving to you from the other side of your computer screen.

But when she looked up, Sam was still scanning her face. "Should I be jealous?"

Emma blinked at him. "Of Michael?"

"You said you had a dream about him."

She snorted. "You have half the mothers in this school showering you with gifts and blushing like teenagers—and you wonder if *you* should be jealous?"

"So, is that a yes?"

She tilted her head, exasperated. "The dream wasn't about Michael, Sam. It was about, well… *me*."

He looked at her with narrowed eyes.

"I'm serious." She fanned out her hands over his chest, clearing off a few more sprays of flour with her fingertips. "It was just one of those weird dreams. Michael was sort of showing me things from my past. Kind of like in *A Christmas Carol.*"

"So Michael was a ghost?"

"More like… a tour guide."

Sam nodded slowly. Emma watched his expression, relieved to see the suspicious crease in his brow begin to loosen, his forehead growing smooth again, signaling she'd satisfied his curiosity—and, hopefully, his concern. "Then, in that case, follow me." He took her hand and led her past the spirited chaos of the kids cooking and through the kitchen doors to where a brown bag sat on the counter. "Dinner, as promised," he said, handing it to her.

She took the heavy bag and gently unfolded the top, releasing a warm, spicy whiff of his promised fish curry. "This smells amazing."

"The rice is in a separate container so it doesn't get too soupy."

She lowered the bag and stepped closer, the comforting heat she'd enjoyed earlier in his embrace deepening. She scanned his face, thinking how warm his mouth would feel on hers. "I'd show you the extent of my gratitude," she whispered, "but I'm worried we might end up in the principal's office."

Sam's hands came around her waist and pulled her closer. It was all she could do not to melt against him like a caught snowflake. "I'm willing to risk it if you are," he whispered. "I hear he goes easy on first-time offenders."

"Who says it would be my first time?" she teased.

"Well, well. I didn't know I was dating a reformed delinquent. Sexy."

She laughed as his palms scaled her spine. "Not quite," she confessed. "The only thing I ever got in trouble for in school was overdue books."

Sam dropped his forehead against hers, his breath suddenly ragged. "Sure I can't convince you to take a break later tonight and let me bring over some dessert?"

"Let me guess"—Emma bit her lip in playful deliberation—"cookies?"

He grinned as he leaned in. "I promise no broken ones."

When his mouth closed over hers, Emma arched into his chest, letting the heat of his lips travel through her.

Drawing back to catch her breath, she laughed against his mouth. "Or any with dinosaur chunks?"

"That," he said, "might be harder to guarantee."

BACK HOME A half hour later, Emma unpacked her dinner, poured herself a glass of red wine, and carried everything to her desk. Looking down at the table, she felt the prickle of dread. If a few spoonfuls of gingerbread ice cream could twist her dreams that badly, she could only imagine the insanity *this* spread would yield.

Who cares? she decided, taking a generous forkful of the creamy dish into her mouth and savoring the peppery, tender fish. It would be worth crazy dreams. Not that she expected to have any. Things between her and Sam were smooth again, harmonious and solid—so her subconscious could feel free to cool off and take her into more familiar dream territory tonight, something forgettable like arriving at a design meeting in her underwear.

Emma was feeling so good, in fact, that she even tapped on a Christmas jazz channel on her tablet and let the deep, sonorous purr of Nat King Cole fill the room.

She recalled her earlier conversation with Vanessa, her best friend's dogged determination to press the subject of a marriage proposal, and suddenly the possibility didn't send pangs of alarm up Emma's arms. Could she blame that on the delicious dinner too?

Whatever ingredients Sam had put in his curry had surely contained a bit of magic, because by eleven thirty, she'd nearly completed her presentation. At least close enough that when her eyes grew heavy, she decided she could allow herself slumber.

But no more falling asleep in her clothes. Instead, she tugged on the oversized tee she wore for a nightgown. Tonight, however, she would add a pair of yoga pants. Just in case.

Chapter Seven

*N*OT AGAIN.

This was Emma's first thought when she sat up in bed at 3:12 a.m. and saw Ethan Avery standing at the foot of her mattress in a collared shirt and khaki slacks, his wavy red hair cut close to his scalp. His smile was as warm and welcoming as the first time he'd flashed it at her across their shared drafting tables at Powder Marketing.

Her second thought was that she'd been smart to remember the yoga pants.

"It's good to see you, Emmy."

It was something to see him too—but Emma wasn't sure *good* was necessarily the right word. Pleasant, maybe. Definitely not surprising, though. If she'd given any thought to a possible successor to Michael as dream-appointed tour guide—not that she had—Emma would certainly have guessed Ethan. Her first boyfriend after college had been solid, almost as much a mother's dream as Sam. When they'd met as interns at Powder Marketing, Emma had been smitten from the start.

"You don't seem surprised to see me," he said, arching

one copper-colored brow at her.

"This isn't my first time," Emma said, then flushed. "Having an ex-boyfriend come back in my dream, I mean," she clarified quickly.

Ethan grinned, a sort of half smirk that used to make her skin prickle. Tonight, however, her skin prickled for another reason. Dread. Ethan had come to continue her journey down memory lane—had she misremembered their breakup as badly as she had her end with Michael?

"You look great," he said.

In a thread-bare T-shirt with wild sleep hair? Yeah, right. He was just buttering her up. No wonder Ethan had moved so quickly up the ranks at Powder while she'd lingered interminably in the trenches of the art department. Had he been as agile winning her affections as he had winning every subsequent promotion?

"I heard about the Johnson account," he said. "Exciting."

"Thanks, but I haven't won it yet."

"You will."

He sounded so sure. But then, it was easy to be sure in a dream, wasn't it? Last night, Emma would have labored over that very question, but tonight, she found herself too relaxed to care—the whole of her, in fact, remarkably calm and easy. Too easy, frankly. Because, while it was a kick seeing Ethan—a man she'd dated nearly two years, and had even considered marrying—in her dream after all these years, she really didn't know why he'd bothered showing up. After today's visit with Sam at the school, she was certain she'd repaired whatever damage she'd done at the restaurant. Surely the dream gods—or whoever *they* were who'd come up with this plan—weren't still worried she was going to ruin the good thing she had with Sam, were they?

And as diverting as these Dickens-inspired dreams were, Emma was hoping for something a little lighter tonight. "Look, Ethan. I appreciate the gesture here—that you're going to show me something to scare me into saving my relationship—but, honestly, it doesn't need rescuing. I mean, yes, the whole showing-up-late-to-dinner thing definitely warranted a good wake-up call, but I saw Sam today, and it's all water under the bridge. We're fine. *Really.*"

She glanced up to gauge Ethan's expression and was startled to find him wearing the same stone-faced stare he used to give the design assistants when they'd try to worm their way out of a deadline. "All I know, Emma, is that I'm supposed to show you a few things—"

"I understand, but that was yesterday. Today things are good."

Still, Ethan remained dubious. "Look, I can double-check to see if they've updated the assignment..." He pulled out his phone, tapped it to life, and scrolled for several seconds before he announced, "Nope. There's no change to the account."

Emma blinked at him. "I have an *account?*"

"Everyone does," he said, stuffing his cell back into his

pocket. "It keeps things organized." He must love that—had Emma forgotten Ethan's obsessive need to constantly tidy up her computer's desktop every time they'd worked together on a project?

She blew out a defeated sigh. *Fine.* She might as well let the dream—and her guide—run their course. After all, unlike her relationship with Michael, Emma's time with Ethan had been much more mature. Surely she wouldn't cringe nearly as much at the scenes Ethan meant to walk her through. At the very least, she decided as the room began to swim with silvery light, she wouldn't have to worry about Ethan jumping onto a chair to serenade an entire coffeehouse with "Jingle Bells."

Chapter Eight

THE SOUNDS OF Christmas music and loud, cheery voices came into clarity shortly before the sight of their old office lobby at Powder Marketing. Emma would never forget when she'd stepped into the space for her first interview, how struck she'd been by the sleekness of it. The blocky white leather couches, the equally unblemished squares of carpet underneath them. And the curved reception area, faced in glossy white laminate, looked more like the bow of a cruise ship than a desk.

Even in dream, Emma marveled at the space, her gaze shifting to scan the wall of glass behind the reception area that revealed the gleeful chaos of what was obviously Powder's office Christmas party.

She scanned the crowds expectantly. "Are you and I in there?"

Ethan shook his head. "We're over there," he said, pointing down the hall in the direction of the design offices.

"Ah." Emma grinned wickedly. "Let me guess—we got sloppy on mulled wine and ran back to the design studio to make out, right?"

Ethan looked at her as if she'd suggested they went skinny-dipping in the lobby fountain. "You don't remember? We were both rushing to finish the Collingswood project."

"We were *working* during the office party?"

"Deadlines don't take holidays, Emma. You told me that."

A sheepish flush crawled up her throat, remembering she'd said the same thing to Vanessa the other day. No wonder Vanessa had glowered at her for it. "Are you saying I didn't come out from my office the entire party?"

"Oh, no, you came out." Ethan nodded to the elevator doors just as they chimed and slid open. A rangy, jean-clad twenty-something guy with a blond buzz cut and a messenger bag slung over his shoulder stepped off and ambled over to the reception desk, where he tapped a buzzer on the tidy surface of the expansive counter.

A few minutes later, Emma emerged from one of the doors in the flanking corridor, dressed in a snug corduroy mini-skirt and riding boots. "Sorry to keep you waiting."

Watching her younger self approach, Emma took a step back reflexively, as if she feared being in her own path—even though she knew that wasn't possible. Last night, she'd been too stunned and confused to do much besides gape at her image the first time she'd seen her double. But now, much like seeing Ethan at the foot of her bed, Emma was getting to be an old pro at this dream stuff.

"Hey, don't worry about it." The bike messenger—who

Emma remembered always thinking was friendly and kind of cute in an alternative-rock kind of way—grinned as he pulled a padded envelope out of his bag and set it on the counter. "Unlike most things, you can actually open this one before Christmas."

As she watched her old self smile at the joke, Emma felt her own lips stretch with amusement too. He *had* been adorable, hadn't he? Clearly her younger version had thought so too.

The guy held out a clipboard for her to sign.

Emma watched their exchange, marveling at her double. "I look different," she whispered, as much to herself as to Ethan.

"Of course you do," said Ethan. "You were eight years younger."

"Not just younger. I mean, I look...I don't know...*softer*."

"Well, you weren't very good about the gym, Emma. I got you that membership at my fitness place, but you were always making excuses—"

"I don't mean like that," she said sharply. "I mean my expression. My posture. My whole demeanor."

Ethan snorted. "It's probably just because you were dizzy from the contact high from whatever Messenger Dude was smoking on the ride over."

Emma cast him a cool glare. "That's awfully judgmental of you."

"Me?" Ethan blinked at her. "*You're* the one who used to point out the way the lobby smelled every time he left."

"I did?" Another burst of regret bloomed hot behind her chest. Why had she been so uptight?

Returning her attention to the scene, Emma saw the cute bike messenger was leaning against the counter and smiling again. "I was kind of hoping I was going to have to crash the party to find someone to sign for this," he said, nodding to the glass partition. "Looks like a great time."

"I wouldn't know," Emma said with a sigh as she handed him back the signed clipboard.

The guy squinted at her. "You're working? On Christmas Eve?"

"Well, so are you."

"Yeah—but only because *you* are." The guy chuckled as he stuffed the clipboard back into his bag. "Just kidding."

Emma felt her own cheeks mirror the flush she watched grow on her double's face at his teasing. "What was that guy's name again?" she asked Ethan.

"Craig."

"He was cute. Funny too."

"He asked you out once," Ethan said, "but luckily for me—and for you—Amy from accounting talked you out of it."

Emma turned to Ethan. "She did?" She could hear the edge of disappointment in her voice, and clearly Ethan had detected it too.

He fixed a disapproving scowl on her. "Oh, come on, Emmy. You with a bike messenger? Seriously?"

She felt a charge of indignation tear up her spine. "It happens to be a real job, Ethan."

"Maybe. But it's not a *career*. At least not one you'd actually want to brag about."

"You don't know that." Emma frowned. Was she honestly arguing with a dream?

Futile or not, Ethan seemed keen on continuing the debate. "So, if Sam were to come to you and say he wanted to give up his impressive job at the architecture firm to teach little kids to cook full-time for half the salary, you'd be okay with that?"

She scoffed. "The school wouldn't do that. There's barely enough money from the grants to pay for the supplies."

Ethan hitched his shoulders. "Don't be so sure—budgets can be adjusted."

"But he's worked hard for that spot at the firm. Why would he give that up to get splattered with frosting all day?"

"Who knows?" Ethan reached up to smooth the sides of his short red hair and shrugged. "Maybe the same reason Craig is still tearing around the streets of Boston on that goofy bike—because he loves it."

Needing clarification, Emma turned her gaze back to the reception desk, but the scene was already fading, the sound of piped Christmas carols growing muffled and soft. Like last night, she suspected the blurring signaled the end of the dream and expected to find Ethan gone when she turned, but he remained beside her, his expression suddenly grave.

She felt a twinge of dread. "Why do I think we're not done yet?"

Chapter Nine

UNTIL THE INTERIOR of Calla's Restaurant came into focus, the familiar smells of sautéed onions and seared tuna emerging with the view, Emma wasn't sure which part of their last evening together Ethan meant to show her. Truth be told, even now, popped back into the scene, Emma struggled to recall the exact setting of their unraveling. The night itself had been long—she definitely remembered *that*—on the heels of a day filled with much excitement— nearing the end of her long tenure as a part-time design assistant, Emma had been awarded a full-time position in the agency. Which was why, when Ethan had announced they were going out to dinner, Emma had assumed it had been to celebrate her new job.

"This is where we broke up, isn't it?" she asked, scanning the crowded restaurant. "You want to remind me how you dumped me, right?"

Ethan, looking suddenly exasperated, pointed her to a table in the back where their doubles were taking their seats. "Just watch, okay?"

THEIR WAITER ARRIVED with a bottle of champagne.

Emma caught a quick look at the label before the man turned it to Ethan for his approval.

"You didn't need to be so extravagant," she said, watching the sparkling, golden-hued liquid poured into their flutes. "I would have been happy toasting my promotion with merlot."

"I thought this much good news deserved something more than the house red," Ethan said, nodding for the waiter to set the bottle into the chilled bucket beside them.

"What do you mean?" Emma looked at him. "There's more than just my new job?"

Ethan scooped up his glass and gestured for her to do the same. "First we toast," he said, tipping his champagne toward hers. "To what's next."

An auspicious choice of words, Emma couldn't help thinking as she joined Ethan in a celebratory sip. The burst of effervescence tickled her nose and quickly sent a pulse of warmth rushing through her chest. "And just what *is* next?" she asked then tilted her flute at him for emphasis. "And don't say appetizers."

Ethan set down his glass, his blue eyes darkening to gray. "They want me in the Charlotte office."

Emma stared at him as the news sank in. She'd been looking forward to toasting her new job and before she could take a second celebratory sip of champagne, Ethan had just informed her he was leaving Boston and moving to North Carolina.

When she remained mute, he leaned in, visibly impatient. "Say something, Emmy."

"I—I don't know what to say," she stammered.

"You could start with congratulations."

She could. And she *was* happy for his success, of course she was, but surely he understood that there were other things to consider in the wake of this announcement.

"Congratulations," she said, somehow mustering a cheerful tone as she raised her glass for yet another toast.

"Wait, don't put it down yet," Ethan said when she lowered her flute.

A prickle of dread fluttered across her scalp. There was more?

"We make a great team, Emmy. You know we do."

Was he serious? She cast him a cool look. "You mean, we *did.*"

Ethan's pale eyes narrowed quizzically. "You misunderstand… I want us to get married."

"Married?" Now it was her turn to look bewildered. "But you're moving to Charlotte."

"We'd move down there together—*obviously*." He chuckled and sat back. "I'm on the fence about long-distance relationships, but I definitely draw the line at long-distance *marriage*."

"But I have a job here, Ethan."

"I know, I know." He put up his hands, as if trying to calm a charging. "And don't worry, I already spoke with Peter in the Charlotte office and he says he could definitely find you a spot in the art department there. It's entry-level, but at least it would be in your field," he said, his gaze flickering expectantly over her face in the heavy silence that followed.

Was he honestly waiting for her to show some kind of gratitude?

Her pulse hastened. "Ethan, I've been offered a promotion *here*. One I've worked very hard for. Why would I throw that away to start at the bottom again?"

His face fell at her question. "Because you'd be with me," he said, his voice tinged with hurt and something else—a slight edge of outrage. Good grief—he *had* expected her to be grateful to him! "Emma, are you saying you don't want to be with me?"

"Of course I do. But if this is about us being together, why can't we just stay here?"

The waiter arrived to take their orders, forcing them to halt their debate and soften their strained features with polite smiles while they selected their meals, though Emma had suddenly lost her appetite.

But when their waiter retreated, Ethan leaned forward to continue his pitch. "I'll be making more money in Charlotte, Emmy."

"What about the good money *I* make here?"

Ethan swept up his drink and sat back. He swirled his champagne, his gaze fixed harshly on his glass, his voice flat. "I knew you'd do this."

"Do what?"

"I'm asking you to move to Charlotte with me—and you're acting like I'm trying to force you to give up your job."

She folded her arms. "Because you *are*. Saying you've secured me some entry-level job isn't exactly sweetening the deal for me. I've worked hard to get where I am."

Ethan's eyes rose to meet hers. "This is about your mom, isn't it?"

Emma's forehead flushed with heat. She reached for her ice water and downed a long sip, hoping the frigid liquid would cool her outrage. It didn't work.

She set down her glass. "You don't understand."

"Then help me to," Ethan pressed. "Emma, I've met your mother. She seems like a pretty contented person to me."

"Who's completely dependent on my father. My mother worked just as hard taking care of our house as my father did at the bank. Yet she still felt bad asking him for ten dollars to get her hair cut because he made her feel that way. As if it wasn't her money to spend."

"So, you just assume if we get married and you don't make as much as I do then I'll do the same thing to you?"

She chewed her lip, not sure about anything anymore. Only that this dinner had taken a very wrong turn—and she wasn't sure any map could get them back on course.

"I won't apologize for wanting to have my own money, Ethan."

"Am I asking you to?"

She set down her utensils and sat back, letting her hands fall into her lap. "Maybe I just don't understand why I have to be the one to leave my job."

"Emmy, I got a promotion."

"So did I, Ethan."

They stared at one another across the table, the boom of a stalemate painfully loud in the silence, but it was Ethan who took it upon himself to cement their fate with words.

"Or maybe there's another reason you don't want to come with me, and you're not saying it."

"Which is?"

"That you would be willing to make this move, to take this chance, for the right guy."

Emma lowered her gaze to her lap, unable to answer—all the while knowing that with every second of silence that followed while Ethan waited for her to contest, his theory gained weight.

Looking up to last to meet Ethan's strained eyes, she saw he knew it too.

He slapped his napkin on the table. "I'll find our waiter and cancel our order."

Chapter Ten

WHILE THE SCENE faded before her eyes, Emma flung her hands out into the dimming fog, as if trying to grab the blurring pieces before they disappeared completely. When they had and she found the familiar imagery of her room coming into focus in their place, Ethan was still beside her.

She looked up at him. "I can't believe you just *left*."

"Were we watching the same scene just now?" Ethan squinted at her as if she'd just asked him to explain the difference between the sun and the moon. "I think it was pretty obvious you didn't want to come with me."

"Because you made me choose," she said, hearing her voice growing shrill. "You or my career!"

The familiar ping of an incoming text message sounded, and Emma glanced around the room for her phone.

Ethan raised his hand to stop her search. "That'll be me," he said, freeing his phone. He tapped the screen, scanned it, then returned his cell to his pocket. "Afraid I have to head out—I just got assigned to the dreams of my cousin Eddie. You met him at my cousin's wedding in Philly. Apparently, he's thinking about relocating to Iceland and needs a little reminding of how well the last move he made went."

Watching him turn toward the door, Emma felt a curious burst of panic. Parting from Michael last night had been easy—relieving, really, as if she'd survived some dreaded dentist appointment and couldn't wait to rush home to down a pint of ice cream. But tonight she felt an urgency in seeing Ethan depart, as if there was still more he needed to reveal. "Ethan, wait," she said.

At the door, he turned back to face her, his features once again strained with impatience. "Emmy, if you're going to watch these scenes and not *see* them, there's really no point. I'm just here to show you things—it's your job to figure them out."

"Are you saying I screwed up by not moving to Charlotte with you? Is that it?" She searched his weary eyes. "Are you saying we might have had a shot?"

"Look. You want to remember our breakup your way, but the truth is, it didn't have anything to do with your parents or me forcing you to make a choice about your job. I just wasn't the right guy." His eyes pooled with something so close to disappointment that Emma took a step back.

"So you're saying…what? Sam *is*?"

Another alert chimed from the pocket where he'd stashed his phone. "Sorry. Lower-level dream guides aren't authorized to give spoilers. Besides…" He tilted his head toward the other side of the room, where her computer blinked suddenly to life, the screen glowing with her nearly-complete mockup. "You've got a career-making presentation to finish."

Chapter Eleven

WHILE EMMA HAD suffered a few wine hangovers in her time, until this morning, she'd never had a dream hangover—but that was definitely what she was going to call the relentless throbbing that greeted her when she woke, and was still keeping her company as she walked— albeit slightly unsteadily—into her office at nine thirty.

The only thing that kept her upright was the fact that somewhere between Ethan's visit and the piercing light of dawn, she'd finished her presentation and emailed it to Diane for review. And best of all, she felt great about it. Sure, some of the designs still needed a little polishing, but the basic concepts were there—and Diane would want to put her own stamp on it, even if it *was* perfect.

Back in her cubicle, Emma's phone chimed with a new text. Picking it up, her pulse hastened; she was sure it was Diane notifying her that she'd looked at Emma's designs and made her decision. But a message from Sam blinked on her screen instead, filling her with a warm surge of affection as she read his message. *"Good morning, sunshine. Sleep better last night?"*

"Define better," Emma replied.

"Okay. Any more reunions with old boyfriends I should know about?"

Emma smiled as she typed back. *"That depends—any more adoring mothers bearing gift bags I should know about?"*

"Very funny. Did you finish the presentation?"

"YES. Diane's reviewing it now. I'M. A. WRECK."

"Phew. Otherwise I was going to have to get a refund on the Lear jet I rented to celebrate tonight after the packing party."

Emma laughed, another burst of relief filling her. With her presentation finished, she wouldn't have to worry about missing tonight's event at the school—*or* being unable to leave with Sam for his parents' house tomorrow morning as they'd planned. She'd spent the last few days anticipating panic and swallowing dread; now she could finally enjoy peace.

As wild and unsettling as the dreams of the last two nights had been, maybe there *had* been something magical in their visions. Not that Emma planned to admit that out loud...

"Emma?"

She glanced up to find Diane's assistant, Sandra, filling her cubicle doorway. Heat flooded her cheeks as she set her phone facedown.

"Diane wants to see you in her office."

Emma's heart thudded against her chest. Even as she climbed out of her chair and gave her skirt a fortifying tug and her ponytail a quick smoothing, an inner debate raged.

A rejection would have been easily done over email, yes? But then, Diane was notorious for taking pleasure in cutting down her artists' work in person, so this request for Emma to come to her office didn't necessarily mean good news, either.

Walking around her desk, she glanced at Sandra, seeking clues in the younger woman's expression but finding none in her Sphinx-like smile.

Emma shrugged, infusing her voice with a good-natured attitude she most certainly didn't feel as she swallowed hard and said, "Wish me luck."

SHE HATED IT.

This was Emma's first thought when she came into Diane's office and met with her boss's unsmiling face. Emma felt sure all the blood had drained to her ankles.

"Have a seat," the woman said, pointing her stylus to the two upholstered chairs on the other side of her desk, and Emma was grateful to sink into one, suddenly aware her legs had turned to rubber.

Waiting in the crackling and interminable silence as Diane finished a text, Emma fought to keep her smile high and optimistic, despite the thoughts of defeat that screamed through her thoughts.

I've poured my heart and soul into these designs, and she hates them.

So she'd get another shot, Emma told herself as the quiet endured. She'd feel good about her efforts and, most especially, she wouldn't let this drag down her whole holiday. It was just one account, right? She could put this away and still enjoy Christmas...*right?*

"They're brilliant."

Emma blinked at Diane, her boss's decree snapping her back from her self-pitying musings.

Had she said *brilliant?*

"They are?" Emma winced at the crack in her voice and tried again, infusing her tone with confidence. "They are," she said again, this time as statement, not question. "Good. I thought so too."

"Simon's first pass was too serious, too self-important," Diane said, tapping the end of her stylus thoughtfully on her bottom lip. "One might even say, *adversarial.* But these are light. Warm. Casual. Today's cooks don't want to feel judged every time they make a meal," Diane said. "They just want permission to enjoy themselves. They want fun, not fuss. Take me, for example. I spent three hundred dollars on a pan designed to sear filet mignon, and do you know how many times I've used it, Emma?"

Emma shook her head patiently.

"Once," Diane said proudly. "And do you know what I cooked in it?"

Emma didn't even dare guess.

"A hot dog!" Diane announced. "A lousy hot dog. *So.*"

She lunged forward and placed both palms on her desk, as if she were planning some kind of Olympic-worthy vault. She fixed Emma with a leveled stare. "Here's the deal. I just got off the phone with Johnson's CEO, Morris Johnson. His flight to St. John's leaves at eight, so he wants you to present to him at seven from his limo on the way to the airport."

Emma felt sure someone had just stepped on her chest.

The squeak she'd worked so hard to remove from her voice earlier returned. "Seven o'clock *tonight?*"

"No, seven o'clock next year." Diane fixed a withering stare on her. "Is that a problem?"

"No," Emma blurted out. "No, that's...that's *great.*" But when she stood up, her legs felt boneless, so rubbery, she feared tripping on her exit.

Fortunately, Diane's eyes were already elsewhere. "Close the door on your way out," her boss said as she tapped into her phone. "Oh, and try not to stare at his hair plugs."

VANESSA WAS WAITING for Emma in her cubicle, her coworker's dark eyes huge behind her lilac-rimmed glasses. "So?"

Emma fell into her chair, amazed she made it down the hall without puddling. She reached for her coffee and took a long, fortifying gulp before answering. "You want the good news or the bad news?"

"Definitely the good," Vanessa said.

"Diane liked my ideas."

"That's fantastic!"

"Yes, it is," Emma said, almost as much to herself as to Vanessa—because it *was*, right? It was amazing news. However. "She liked them *so* much, in fact," Emma added, "that she wants me to present them to their marketing director tonight before he leaves to spend Christmas in St. Johns."

"No way!" Vanessa's eyes narrowed suddenly. "Wait." Her voice quieted, softening suddenly with caution. "Just so I'm clear…we're still in the good-news portion of this conversation, right?"

Emma scrunched up her face. "Tonight is Sam's packing party for the Christmas Cookie Basket Brigade."

"*Oh*." Vanessa's high smile dropped. "So what did Diane say?"

"What do you mean?"

Vanessa dipped her chin, her eyes searching Emma's expectantly. "When you told her you couldn't because you already had plans—what did she say?"

Emma blinked at her. She loved her coworker to pieces, but had Vanessa lost her mind?

"Of course I didn't do that," she said, lowering her voice just in case her boss happened to have abandoned her boots to do some barefoot sneaking-up—it wouldn't have been the first time. "Ness, this is a career-making account we're talking about. Diane wants to know I'm willing to commit, to making this job my priority. You think I'm going to tell her I can't make it because I have to go pack Christmas cookies with a hoard of eight-year-olds?"

"Maybe she could present them for you," Vanessa suggested then added with a wry smirk. "We both know she'll end up taking the credit for your ideas *anyway*."

Diane would, yes, but that wasn't the point. "I have to be there," Emma said firmly. "I *want* to be there."

Vanessa crossed her arms and sat back, her lips pursing pointedly. "I thought you *wanted* to be there for Sam this time."

"I *do*, but—"

"But Sam will understand, right?"

Memories of her visit from Ethan—her *dream*, Emma corrected herself impatiently; she really had to stop acting as if these food-induced hallucinations were actually real—flashed back, but Emma tamped them down. She smoothed the sides of her ponytail, feeling a contrite flush crawl up her neck.

Her friend's eyes narrowed to slits. "I know this account seems like a once-in-a-lifetime gig, but Sam's kind of a once-in-a-lifetime guy. Trust me. I speak from experience."

The hint of distress that Vanessa had worn on her features two days ago had returned—but this time, Emma wouldn't allow the moment to pass unchecked.

She reached across the desk and laid her hand over her

friend's. "I know it sucks being alone during the holidays, Ness—but you did the right thing breaking up with Daniel. He didn't deserve you."

"Thanks for saying that." Her smile rose slightly. "I just want a crystal ball, you know? I want someone to show me my life a year from now so I can know what amazing guy is going to make me glad I broke up with him."

Emma chuckled low. "Try sleeping."

Her coworker tilted her head quizzically. "Sleeping?"

She lowered her hands to her lap and raised her eyes to meet Vanessa's. "You'll think I'm nuts."

"Too late for that." Her coworker grinned, her tightly threaded arms unfolding.

Emma exhaled, the knot of tension between her shoulder blades loosening with her breath. "The last two nights, I've been having these dreams…" She paused, daring to look up to gauge Vanessa's expression.

"Dreams?"

"I think when you joked that I was turning into Ebenezer Scrooge, my subconscious snagged on that."

"So you've been seeing ghosts in your dreams?"

"Not ghosts. Exes."

Once again, Vanessa's mouth crept up into a wry smile. "Is there a difference?"

It was a fair point—and one that brought a much-needed chuckle from Emma's throat. Didn't everyone find themselves haunted by failed relationships? At least Emma's had the decency to plague her while she slept.

"Look," said Vanessa, "if you really *are* getting schooled by your ex-boyfriends in your dreams, then maybe you should listen them. God knows you don't listen to *me*."

When Vanessa stood to leave, Emma's need to clarify her position rose with equal speed. "I know this sounds crazy, but I'm doing this for Sam and me. I want to be sure I'm my own person, with my own means, before I attach myself to someone. I don't want to feel trapped."

She braced for another argument, but Vanessa's face softened with surrender. "I'm not sure any amount of money will protect you from that, but okay."

"One more delay tonight, and then I'm Sam's for the whole holiday. I promise."

"I'm not the one you need to convince, Emma. Then again, I'm not sure Sam is either."

When Vanessa had exited, Emma swung her chair around to snatch her phone and tapped it to life, her pulse racing with excitement as she typed a text to Sam.

"GREAT NEWS!!! Diane loved my designs!! Presenting them to head of marketing after work. Might be a few minutes late to the packing party, but I'LL BE THERE!!!"

She took a moment to reread the text before hitting send, telling herself that by putting her promise in all caps, there was no way she could break it.

Chapter Twelve

F OR THIRTY MINUTES, Morris Johnson hadn't stopped smiling. From the minute Diane had connected the call with Johnson Cookware's CEO at seven ten, the narrow-faced man had been flashing his capped teeth without pause. Then again, Emma wasn't sure her own plastered smile had dimmed for the entirety of their Skype call either.

Even her boss had smiled more in their half-hour phone call than Emma had seen in five years working at Zenith.

"Where have you been hiding this one, Di?" Morris asked.

"I'd tell you, Morrie, but then I'd have to kill you. Just kidding."

Emma glanced at the time stamp on the bottom of the screen—7:40—and her breath caught with relief. She still had plenty of time to get to the cookie packing party. Everyone knew these kinds of events never started on time and always ran over—and just think of all they'd have to celebrate when she got there! She had no doubt her phone had been thrumming quietly for the past hour where she'd buried it in her purse back in her cubicle, her voicemail and text message threads filling with eager words from Sam.

"Here's what I want…" Morris's deep voice brought Emma back to earth. "I'll be having a late breakfast with our VP tomorrow at ten, and I'd like you both to call in so I can conference the updated presentation from the restaurant."

"We can make that happen." Diane swung her gaze to meet Emma's, her dark eyes like lasers. "Right, Emma?"

Emma swallowed, somehow *miraculously* managing to keep her smile intact as she did, which was no easy feat considering she was certain her heart was going to stop at any second. Ten was the time she and Sam were scheduled to leave for his parents' house.

Calm down. Breathe. It would only mean they'd hit the road a few minutes late, that was all. Surely Sam wouldn't be upset over a few—

"So that's one o'clock our time, right, Morris?"

Emma's gaze snapped to Diane, panic sizzling. She'd completely forgotten about the time difference.

Remembering her face was visible to Morris, Emma dipped her chin quickly to hide her nervous flush and waited a beat before raising it again, enough time to cloak her sinking stomach with an agreeable smile that, if stretched any wider, would earn her a stand-in spot for the Joker.

She swallowed. Hard. "I can't wait."

EMMA TOLD HERSELF it was just a lull when she arrived to find the school's snow-dusted parking lot nearly empty at eight ten, that there had surely been an initial rush of guests, but seeing as it was a drop-in event—which, in her experience, always ebbed and flowed in volume—there was no reason to worry that she'd missed the packing party entirely.

Until she reached the front double doors and found them both locked. Then the pangs of dread sparked in earnest.

Emma yanked, hard enough that she hoped the reverberations would echo down the barren—but blessedly still lit—hallway she could see through the doors. At the very least Sam would hear her, wouldn't he? After all, his car was still in the parking lot. Exiting from her meeting, she'd dreaded checking her phone, sure there would be a dozen frantic messages from Sam waiting for her, but to her shock, there hadn't been a single one—and the lack had left her jittery with worry. What did it mean that he hadn't even tried to call?

She tugged harder.

After another few minutes—and a stint of rapping on the glass when Emma grew weary of yanking—a woman with a topknot of frizzy brown hair appeared, dressed in a long wool coat and carrying a stack of empty cookie sheets under her arm.

Emma stepped back, relief crackling through her ribcage. When the woman opened the door, Emma didn't allow her a chance to speak first before she pleaded, "I'm looking for Sam Cole."

"He's still in the kitchen cleaning up," the woman said, pulling on her other glove as she stepped past her and exited into the chilly night before Emma could ask for further directions. Left alone in the foyer, Emma scanned both sides of the hallway, wishing she'd paid more attention when Sam had led her to the cafeteria kitchen the day before. She caught the faint hum of Christmas carols from her left and decided to follow the sound, grateful to hear the jazzy rendition of "Jingle Bells" growing louder, signaling she'd made the right choice. The sticky, sweet smell of frosting and warm sugar cookies still hung in the air as she hurried down the hall, too rushed this visit to savor the festive decorations lining the corridor that she'd enjoyed her last time here.

Only when she approached the propped open double doors to the cafeteria did she realize the distinct lack of children's voices. In fact, despite two signs for the night's party that still flanked the entrance, the only conversation Emma heard was from a handful of adults inside.

She reached up to smooth her ponytail, wishing her heart would slow, but it seemed the closer she drew to the small crowd of people working around a long table at the back of the wide room, the faster her pulse raced. She scanned the group, not finding Sam in the mix. Then he appeared through the kitchen doors, sharing a laugh with a young woman with waves of curly auburn hair that she was stuffing into a beret as they walked.

Watching them together, Emma felt a strange dread fist around her heart and slowed her advance until the woman left his side. When Sam looked up and saw her across the cafeteria, his smile dimmed, quickly enough that Emma had a sudden fear he might change his mind and walk in the other direction.

Not wanting to give him the chance, she picked up her pace, her apology already in motion even before she reached him. "I know I'm late—"

"You're not late." His voice was as stiff as his posture and as frosty as his eyes, which seemed determined not to meet hers but fell instead on a collection of forgotten paper plates and plastic cups that littered the table behind them. "Late is a half hour. Late is when there are still people here. You flat-out missed it, Emma."

Hearing him use her full name filled her with even more apprehension than his chilly gaze.

A man with a graying goatee clapped a hand on Sam's shoulder as he walked past. "Great night, Sam."

"Thanks for your help, Ted," Sam said, offering the man a grateful smile that Emma hoped would remain when Sam returned his gaze to her.

No such luck.

The image of Michael sitting alone in their college coffeehouse flashed suddenly through her mind. Sam's face looked equally drawn with disappointment. Emma felt sick to her stomach.

"I just assumed it would run long," she confessed weakly as she trailed behind him, hoping he would slow his work, but Sam continued to gather empty cups and plates off the tables.

"This isn't some gallery opening, Emma," he said, stuffing his stack of frosting-and-sprinkle-streaked plates into an already-overflowing trash can. "These are little kids. They have to be in bed. When the invitation says the party stops at eight, it stops at eight."

It was obvious this latest infraction would take more than a few absolving smiles to repair, but Emma didn't see the harm in at least trying the healing powers of humor. She moved in close and whispered, "Does this mean I don't get a ride in my Lear jet?"

At last Sam slowed, but only long enough to shoot her a nonplussed glare.

Another memory flashed—this one from her most recent dream with Ethan, his expression on the other side of the dinner table when she couldn't give him an answer to his proposal—and again, Emma shoved the image back, a pang of frustration arriving. "Don't you at least want to talk about how it went?"

"It went great," Sam said, gesturing roughly to the nearly empty room around them before slapping his palm against his forehead. "Oh, wait. I'm sorry. We were talking about *you*, right? What was I thinking?"

The sarcasm in his voice cut deep. If he was this mad about her late arrival, how would he take the news that she'd have to delay their departure tomorrow? Already waist-deep in hot water, she decided she might as well submerge herself entirely. "Sam, we have to talk about tomorrow…"

"Yeah, we do." With no more plates to clear, he stopped and brushed his hands clean on the sides of his jeans. Something in the lowered register of his voice made Emma's pulse race. "I think it's best if you don't come with me."

Relief bloomed in her lungs, so briskly that Emma felt her lips stretch into a smile to let the heartened breath free as quickly as possible. "That's exactly what I was thinking too! You see, the CEO loves my designs but he wants to have the VP see them tomorrow, so Diane and I will need to present to him at one, so I thought you could go ahead to your folks and I'll drive up after the presentation—"

"Emma, you're not hearing me." The edge of resolve she'd detected earlier in Sam's voice had hardened to steel. "I mean I don't want you coming *period.*"

She stiffened, as if someone had laid an icy hand on her spine.

This was bad. This was very, very bad.

Despite her best efforts to keep her voice strong, it came out quivering. "Sam, look. If you need some time…"

"What I *need* is a girlfriend I can count on. A partner. You see all that?" He pointed to the two tables on the edge of the room, covered with all the finished cookie baskets that now awaited delivery tomorrow. "Those are ready to go because all these people here tonight came through. Every one of them had to miss something to be here to help—but they chose to make this a priority. People I barely know kept their word and came. And yet the one person I know better than anyone couldn't be bothered."

Emma rolled her lips together, knowing she should have felt only the heat of contrition, but frustration continued to swell. "That's not fair—I'm doing all of this for *us*."

"You don't want this for us, Em. You want this for *you*."

"We've talked about this. I don't want us to end up like my parents. I don't want to be my mother, so dependent on you that you end up resenting me."

"This isn't about your mother."

She scanned his eyes, her heart thundering.

"This big fear of not being financially dependent on me is just an excuse. Admit it—you're afraid to make the commitment to me. The same way you were afraid to make the commitment to any guy. You just use your mom as an excuse."

Before Emma could volley back another defense—or at least attempt to come up with one—an older man walked through the cafeteria doors and waved to Sam.

"I have to go," he said, moving to meet the man at the side exit.

"Sam, wait!"

When he didn't, just pushed through the door and

joined the man outside instead, Emma hurried across the cafeteria and out the same door. Sam and the man stood in the parking lot, talking next to a white delivery van. The air was noticeably frostier than it had been when she'd first arrived—or maybe it was just the cold of Sam's reaction that was making Emma shiver uncontrollably under her coat as she made her way toward them, hearing their conversation. It didn't help that flurries had started to fall, tiny flakes that would have made Emma would feel warm and comforted on any other night so close to Christmas Day, but somehow tonight the tiny crystals seemed only to chill her more.

"It's supposed to do this off and on all night," the man said, glancing up at the falling snow as he rubbed his hands together, "but we should be fine for tomorrow's delivery."

Sam smiled at him. "Great. We really appreciate this, Fred."

Emma slowed sheepishly as she approached, knowing she had no business expecting Sam to turn his focus to her after their exit in the cafeteria. Still she hoped he might give her another chance. She'd wait.

"I'm afraid I'll be on the road tomorrow morning," Sam told him, "but if you need anything, you can call Gail Weatherly, okay?"

Recognition sparked at the name. The mother of the little boy she'd met the night before. The one with the gift bag and the schoolgirl smile. Sam was depending on *her*? Emma pulled in a sharp breath, the blade of his words a deep cut.

Her heart shivered with it. Why wasn't she the one he turned to?

"Sounds good," Fred said, shaking Sam's hand. "Merry Christmas." He turned to Emma. "And Merry Christmas to you too, miss."

Despite feeling as if she could cry, Emma managed a cheerful smile. "Thank you," she said. "You too."

She and Sam stood in silence while Fred climbed into his van and drove out of the parking lot. Alone again, Emma turned to Sam, sure he didn't mean to leave things this way.

When he moved to leave without a word, Emma rushed after him. "Sam?"

"It's late, Em," he said, continuing to walk to his car. "You should get home before the roads get slick." The edge of anger was gone from his voice, replaced now by a resigned defeat that Emma decided was much worse. At least when he'd been angry, there'd been fight in him. "I sure hope it was worth it."

"It was," she said. "That's what I'm trying to tell you. I got the account."

Sam tugged open the driver's door. "Then I guess you got exactly what you wanted for Christmas. I wish I could say the same."

"Sam—"

"Merry Christmas, Emma."

Sam climbed in and she stepped back while the car engine roared to life. Then, frozen with shock, she stood in the nearly empty parking lot and watched Sam's taillights flicker through the thickening snowfall until they disappeared out of sight.

Chapter Thirteen

EMMA COULDN'T SLEEP. So by three a.m., tired of trying, she threw off the sheets she'd managed to twist into a restless tangle and padded into the kitchen for water. The disastrous ending to her otherwise triumphant day looped through her thoughts.

There was, however, one silver lining to the day's failures—at least she'd been spared the added insult of yet one more ghost dream—

"It's Emma, right?"

Emma's glass slipped from her hand, toppling over onto the counter. She whirled around and stared at the blond man in running shorts and a T-shirt standing in the doorway of her bedroom.

"It *is* Emma, isn't it?" he asked.

"No," she whispered firmly. Was the dream police kidding with this? Sending her *Corey*? The guy she'd rebounded with after breaking up with Ethan? They'd barely dated a month!

"No, it's not Emma?"

"Yes, I'm Emma," she clarified hotly. "*No*, I'm not in the

mood for this tonight."

Corey snorted. "*You're* not?" He threw up his hands. "How do you think *I* feel? I was on the treadmill talking to this gorgeous woman and I was *this close* to getting her number when *poof!* They send me here." Corey picked up Emma's pay stub off the counter, his eyes growing big as he scanned it. "Whoa, I wish I'd known you made this kind of money when we went out—I would have let you buy dinner those times."

"Actually, you did," Emma said tightly, recalling how he'd conveniently forgotten his wallet at every meal. "Let's cut to the chase, okay?" She'd indulged in polite small talk with Michael and Ethan, but two exes into this and she was done with formality. Especially in light of the evening's events. "My boyfriend dumped me tonight, so whatever you have scheduled for me, don't bother, okay?"

"Yeah, I know. I saw the whole thing on the replay. *Ouch.*" He winced like he'd been stung by a bee. Emma glared at him. "Unfortunately, though, once an account is scheduled, it has to be fulfilled. Kind of like a prescription of antibiotics. You gotta take the weeks' worth of pills, even if you're feeling better."

Emma folded her arms and blew out an impatient breath. "So are you the virus or the cure in this scenario?"

Corey snorted and wagged his finger at her. "You're a funny girl. I remember that about you now." A slow, sugges-tive grin started to rise on one side of his mouth. "I also remember you had this cute little mark on your—"

"*Look.* I don't understand why you're here. You and I barely knew each other. We dated for a month—it's hardly enough to bother revisiting."

"Which is exactly why they wanted me to be the last one," said Corey, starting to rummage through her cabinets. "You don't have any, like, chips or crackers or anything, do you?"

"Nope. Fresh out," Emma said tightly. "And what do you mean, that's why they wanted you to be the last?" Three "ghosts" in, and Emma no longer wondered—or cared— who "they" were.

"Because I'm here to show you your past with Stan."

"It's *Sam.*"

"Sam, Stan—whatever." When Emma frowned at him, Corey rolled his eyes and pushed out an exasperated breath. "Hey, listen, *you* try remembering twenty-five names in one night, okay?"

Worry knotted in Emma's throat. Did Corey, did *they,* really mean to twist the knife by making her revisit her early days with Sam? It wasn't enough that her ribs felt like they'd been squeezed in a giant fist, she also needed the added torture of being reminded how wonderful things had been when she and Sam had started dating?

Schedule or not, surely the guy could be reasoned with. Emma stepped closer. "Corey, listen—"

He held out his palm to stop her. "Don't even bother.

It's like—"

"Antibiotics," Emma repeated warily. "I got it. But let's skip the preshow chitchat, okay? My heart already feels like a cracked phone screen; I've got a big meeting tomorrow, and I just want to get this over with."

"Jeez. You sure know how to make a guy feel wanted." Corey waited a beat, maybe to see if she'd soften, but when Emma's gaze remained steely, he shrugged in defeat. "Michael warned me you were a tough nut to crack."

"Excuse me?"

Corey waved his hand. "Never mind. Just follow me to—"

"The door, I know," Emma said dejectedly, already moving toward the foyer.

Chapter Fourteen

I T HAD BEEN snowing the night they'd met; Emma remembered that well. Just a week before Christmas. She also recalled that she'd been ravenously hungry. Trying to meet a deadline for one of the head designers, she'd worked through dinner so that by the time she got off the train at nine-thirty, she was willing to buy food from whatever restaurant was still open.

Fortunately, Sonny's Pizzeria was still serving—or at least Emma hoped they were still open when she saw the restaurant's narrow interior lit from the sidewalk as she stepped out of the station. Coming inside, a bell above the door rang out her arrival. The blast of oven heat on her cold cheeks was as welcoming as the sweet smell of tomato sauce. Colored Christmas lights looped around the counter. A radio atop the display case chimed out a holiday station. A single calzone remained in the case—spinach and ricotta, a young man in a flour-dusted red apron explained. Emma ordered it and took a seat in one of the booths while he heated it up for her, scrolling through her phone to catch up on the handful of emails she'd had to ignore to meet her deadline.

The door rang with a new customer. It was the sound of his voice a few moments later that made Emma look up—deep, with a warm and cheerful quality to it—but it was his smile that kept her staring. Easy and genuine, and flanked by two deep dimples.

"I'll take a calzone to go," he said.

"Sorry, man," the young guy behind the counter said. "Just sold the last one."

Emma dipped her head down, a flush of guilt thawing her chilled cheeks.

The man with the dimples, however, seemed unfazed, Emma decided, sneaking a longer look at him. "No worries," he said, pulling his wallet out of his back pocket. "I'll just take a couple of slices of mushroom."

"Warm 'em up for you?" the server offered.

"Sure." The man turned from the counter, giving Emma a glimpse of his dynamite smile as he walked by to take a seat in the booth across from hers.

The door opened, the bell tinkling as a couple came in.

The handsome man glanced over at the entrance and chuckled. "I'm betting this place hears a lot of angels getting their wings jokes this time of year, what do you think?"

It took Emma a second to realize he was talking to her. She blinked at him quizzically, not getting the joke.

"*It's a Wonderful Life*?" he prompted her. "Every time a bell rings, an angel gets his wings?"

"Oh, right." She offered him a sheepish smirk. "Sorry.

My brain is mush when I'm this hungry."

"Tell me about it. I walked into the dry cleaners next door and tried to order dinner there first."

Emma laughed. "While we're making confessions, I have to come clean about something too."

"It's okay. I'm no angel, either."

She smiled. "Actually, I was talking about the calzone…" She squinted sheepishly. "I'm afraid I took the last one."

"It's my own fault." He shrugged, his lips rising in another easygoing smile, this one making his blue eyes sparkle. "That's what I get for deciding to add a third story to a two-story model at the last minute. That and a cage match with an ornery X-ACTO knife," he said, lifting his bandaged thumb.

"Ouch." Emma grimaced. "Are you okay?"

"That depends—if I say I'm in excruciating pain and near death, will you give up your calzone out of pity?"

"Not a chance."

He laughed. "Fair enough.

Emma touched her cheek, wondering if the warmth their banter was stirring in her stomach had moved higher up.

He extended his unbandaged hand. "Sam Cole."

"Emma Wallace." She slid her fingers into his warm palm, heat scaling her spine as he met her eyes.

"Is that why you're eating so late too?" he said. "Long night at the office?"

She sighed. "Is there any other kind?"

"So what do you do?"

"I'm a digital designer at an ad agency. My team and I were helping to finish a campaign for a paper towel company."

"I wasn't aware paper towels needed advertising."

"You'd be surprised."

The sound of something being set down drew both of their gazes to the counter, where two plastic bags had appeared.

"That must be us," said Sam.

They rose together and approached the counter. Sure hers was the smaller of the two, Emma grabbed the bag closest to her. "Well." She offered Sam a quick nod. "Enjoy your dinner."

"You too," he said, taking the other bag.

As much as she wanted an excuse to walk out with him, to keep their conversation—and flirtation—going, she'd delayed sustenance and sleep long enough. The air, so heavy with chill when she'd first stepped into the restaurant, didn't seem nearly as prickly on her bare cheeks now. Or maybe it was just that her skin remained flushed with heat from their teasing banter. Starting down the sidewalk, flutters of disappointment took flight in her stomach. She couldn't help wishing he'd asked for her number, or even an email...

"Emma?"

She stopped and turned to find Sam Cole coming out the pizzeria, his takeout bag held out as he walked to meet her.

"You grabbed the wrong one."

She glanced down into her bag, pried open a corner of the container, and found the fragrant points of his pizza slices. "Thanks," she said as they exchanged bags. "I didn't even think to check."

"Just shows how hungry we are, I guess."

Under the warm glow of the streetlamp, his eyes looked nearly turquoise. Emma caught threads of copper in the chestnut hair at his temples. "At least we both get to call it a night now," she said cheerfully.

"I'm afraid I won't get to punch out just yet," Sam said. "I have to swing by the school to clean up my classroom."

She frowned, confused. "You're a *teacher*? I thought you said you were an architect."

"I *am* an architect. But I volunteer at the elementary school one night a week. They have this after-school program where I teach kids to cook."

"An architect *and* a chef."

"Only trained in the former," he said. "I'm self-taught in the latter."

"I see." Emma dipped her chin and shot him a playful look of indignation. "So here I am wracked with guilt for taking that last calzone, and now I find out you could whip one up for yourself in a few minutes?"

Sam squinted. "It might be more like an *hour*, taking the whole yeast-rise into account, but yeah, pretty much." He smiled sheepishly as he scanned her face, his blue eyes flashing with interest. "So you were *wracked* with guilt, huh?"

Emma chuckled. "Okay, maybe not really wracked. Maybe more like...*needled*." She met his teasing eyes and her throat warmed with pleasure. How was this possible? Fifteen minutes earlier, the only thing on her mind had been food and a warm bed to collapse into. Now...

"I should let you get home before that gets cold." Sam pointed to her takeout bag as he turned to go. "Good night—and Merry Christmas."

Watching him start down the sidewalk again, Emma felt a jolt of need, the urge to detain him fierce again. "You do realize you didn't have to tell me," she blurted out.

To her relief, Sam stopped and turned around. "Tell you what?"

"That we took the wrong bags. You could have just let me get home with your slices and then it would have been too late. You'd have had your calzone after all."

"True," Sam said as he came back toward her. "But the bad karma would have been brutal. I'd be looking at months of lost parking spaces, shredded mail, broken eggs. You name it."

She bit back a smile. "And here I thought you were being noble."

"I can't be both?"

They considered each another in the charged silence.

Sam took a step toward her, his voice deepening with inquiry. "I know it's almost Christmas and you've probably got a hundred parties to go to between now and the big day, but I'd love to make you dinner."

Emma's forehead flushed with pleasure at his invitation. The truth was she had been invited to plenty of parties this season, but she'd declined every one in favor of getting her work done. And while there was still plenty to do before her current assignment could be considered complete, Emma didn't see the harm in taking one night off. "I'd love that."

Just when Emma thought she couldn't blush any warmer, Sam's face broke into the gorgeous smile again, and she felt her entire body light.

"Great," he said. "How about tomorrow night?"

Chapter Fifteen

ACCUSTOMED TO THE drill now, Emma waited for the mist to clear before she looked up to find Corey standing beside her, his strained expression falling somewhere between envy and contempt.

He rolled his eyes and snorted. "Guys who use the whole I'm-a-cook thing to try to get chicks are so lame."

"Sam *is* a cook"—had she really dated a guy who used the word *chicks*—"and he wasn't try to *get me*. He was just being himself," Emma defended hotly, scanning the blur around them for a final glimpse of Sam. She'd watched the scene with a smile on her face, one not so unlike the smile she'd seen her old self wearing throughout their entire exchange. In the years since she and Sam had met, she'd always remembered their first encounter fondly, but seeing it freshly, regret churned in her stomach. How obvious it was that they'd had feelings for each other from the start, how easy he was to be around, how she'd found herself wanting to remain in his company all night.

She turned back to Corey, only to find him on the move again, steering them deeper into the silvery fog, and gooseflesh sparked up her arms. Surely, he didn't mean to torture her with more scenes of the two of them falling in love, did he?

Her answer came in the next instant as the wash of white around them sharpened and the interior of Sam's apartment came into painfully crisp clarity. And with it, the peppery, tangy, and all-too-familiar smell of Sam's seafood paella.

Understanding prickled; Corey was going to make her watch their first date, the sadist.

Sam stood in the kitchen, moving deftly from the fridge to the stove to the sink, his brow set with focus but his eyes appearing fraught. Had something gone wrong with his menu?

Emma leaned toward Corey. "He looks concerned," she whispered.

"Of course he's concerned." Corey pointed to the clock on the stove where the green digital numbers shone 7:15. "You should have gotten there fifteen minutes ago."

Emma felt the heat of remorse scald her neck—she'd been late for their first date! She stared furtively at the door, willing her old self to appear and chastising herself more each second she didn't. Why had she made him wait? Rummaging through her memories, Emma couldn't recall. Had it been something at work keeping her? No doubt. But had it really been more important than getting to Sam's on time? He was making her dinner, for goodness sake!

When a knock finally sounded, Emma exhaled.

Sam gave his hands a rough wipe on a dish towel and slung it over his shoulder as he walked to the door. And even as he gripped the knob, turned and pulled, Emma felt her heart racing with the same thundering pace of her twenty-nine-year-old self, waiting on the other side of the door.

"You look nervous," Corey said as they watched Emma follow Sam into his apartment. "Super hot, but nervous."

Emma cast him an unappreciative glare, but the truth was she *had* been nervous. More so than she might have admitted to herself at the time. Now, watching her doppelganger slide onto one of the three stools that hugged the curved breakfast bar, Emma could see the color in her younger self's cheeks. It had been a cold night, she recalled, and a fairly brisk walk from her car, but the pink wasn't from the frigid air. And it wasn't an anxious flush, either—not the kind she often wore when she was preparing for a meeting with a potential design client. It was the heat of desire. Even then Emma had known that Sam was special.

And still she'd made him wait.

"Pretty small place for a hotshot architect," Corey muttered, glancing around Sam's apartment.

Emma had thought the same when she'd first arrived, hadn't she? Yet now, scanning the narrow and sparsely furnished space, Sam's tiny fake tree sitting atop a coffee table in the equally cramped living room, Emma felt a rush of affection for it. How warm it always felt, how it always smelled of some delicious simmering dish. Tremors of longing flickered—would she never get to be there with him again?

"And you'd think he could have afforded a decent tree," Corey added, pointing to the twinkling two-footer, its spindly branches laden with oversized colored bulbs.

"He hated the thought of cutting down a live tree, so he bought a fake one," Emma defended. "It had nothing to do with money." Yet hadn't she assumed the same thing when she'd arrived? Another pang of regret sparked.

"I was going for 'sidewalk chic,'" Sam joked as they took seats around the rickety card table Emma recalled learning later he had found on trash day at the end of his block.

Emma smiled, even as she watched the face of her younger self break into a wide smile too.

"Dude thinks he's a riot, doesn't he?" Corey whispered sourly.

"Shh." Butterflies of anticipation took flight. All the scenes she'd been shown before this one had filled her with a nagging sense of dread—but this night she couldn't wait to savor all over again. "I want to watch."

Chapter Sixteen

EMMA HAD NEVER tasted anything so delicious in her whole life. The saltiness of the shrimp blended with the spice of the saffron and the crisp burst of green with the fresh peas. When she finally looked up from her plate, she found Sam watching her intently, clearly waiting for her review.

"What do you think? Not bad?"

"Are you kidding?" Emma paused to wipe her mouth on the folded paper towel he'd provided as a napkin. "It's incredible."

"I'm glad you think so." Sam smiled as he took a swig of the red wine he'd opened for them. "Paella isn't everyone's taste."

"If this isn't someone's taste, then they *have* no taste," said Emma, delighted to see a grateful smile tease his lips. "So who taught you to cook like this?"

"I taught myself. My folks ran an insurance office and they wouldn't get home sometimes until eight or nine. They'd leave money for dinner, but my younger brothers got tired of pizza pretty fast, so I decided to step it up one night and make lasagna." He offered her an easy shrug. "After that, they wouldn't go back to takeout."

Emma laughed. "What is that phrase? No good deed…"

"Exactly," Sam said, sweeping up his glass and studying her over the rim. "So how about you?"

"How about me what?" Emma asked, feeling her skin warm at his study.

"Do you cook?"

"That depends." She offered him a sheepish smile. "Does heating up leftovers in the microwave count?"

He chuckled. "If that's a subtle hint that you want me to send you home with some for later, I'm glad to."

She smiled. "Am I that transparent?"

"Let me guess—you had parents who worked long hours too?"

"My dad's days were definitely long at the office. So were my mom's. Except she worked keeping our house together. She had a job as a nurse when they married. After I was born, she didn't go back."

"Do you think she missed it?"

"I have to believe she missed *parts* of it," Emma said. "Having her own income, for one thing. My dad was kind of a tightwad with money."

His eyes pooled with tenderness. "I know the type."

"I guess that's why it's so important to me to make my own money, my own way. I don't ever want to feel like I'm beholden to my husband. To feel trapped."

She quieted, feeling a rush of regret. They barely knew

each other and she was confessing something so personal.

She reached for her wine and took a sip, needing an excuse to break away from his warm gaze—and a new subject. "So you never wanted to make a career as a chef?"

"It's a lot harder to please a restaurant full of customers every night than three muddy boys who don't have any choice but to eat what I serve them," he said with a chuckle.

"I'm sure. So why architecture?"

Sam set his elbows on the table and laced his hands over his plate. "I like creating spaces. Helping people to shape their homes. Places that have meaning for them. Community."

"And the work at the school?"

"The same, I suppose. It's about fostering community. Neighborhoods." Sam paused to add more wine to their glasses. "You ask me why I picked one over the other, but I guess I don't see it that way. Just because I don't get paid as a chef doesn't mean I can't still cook for the people I love." At the word, he sat back and cleared his throat, a faint rash of color spreading along his strong jaw. "Or just, you know, *like*."

"Of course," Emma said, feeling her own body warm at the suggestion of their mutual attraction. Scooping up another forkful of the fragrant rice dish, she couldn't help thinking about the men she'd known, men she'd dated. All of them so focused on the spoils of their careers, their own world. Sam's interest in others wasn't just admirable, it was also undeniably sexy.

"Enough about me," he said, taking up his fork again. "How did you get into advertising?"

"Well…" She smiled sheepishly. "Most people like to watch TV for the shows, right? Not me. As a kid, my favorite part was always the commercials."

Sam grinned. "Remind me to never let you have the remote."

She laughed. "What can I say? Figuring out why people want what they want fascinates me."

"Then why not go into psychology?"

"I'm afraid I'm too fond of pretty pictures. But I still love the challenge of it. Looking at the data to see what works and what doesn't work to move the needle of consumer interest in a product. Which campaigns take off and which ones sink like stones."

"So how about me?" Sam leaned in, the suggestive lift of one side of his mouth mimicking the raspy edge of query in his voice. "Have you figured out what I want yet?" he asked low. "Or do you need to see more data?"

She swirled her wine absently, too lost in his smoldering gaze to actually lift the glass to her lips. Not even a sip of good wine was worth blocking his gorgeous blue eyes. "I'm thinking you might be one of those rare customers who doesn't follow trends. Who has to see the proof of a product's worth for himself before he commits."

"I'm glad to hear it. But I have a feeling I might be more

of a wildcard tonight."

"Really?" Emma's pulse hastened. "How's that?"

Sam smiled. "Because I think I'm already sold."

Chapter Seventeen

"*OH WOW...*"

So lost in watching herself and Sam, Emma didn't realize she'd released her smitten sigh out loud until Corey shot her a disparaging scowl. "I don't remember you ever getting gooey on our first date." He huffed.

"That's because our first date was you flirting with our waitress while I went to put more quarters in the meter," Emma fired back then returned her gaze to the action in Sam's apartment, eager to continue—but the scene was already melting from view. Her heart sank. "But I want to see more," she pleaded.

"Sorry, gotta keep moving," Corey said. "And since we're running short on time, these next few memories are going to be more like a montage."

It was an accurate comparison, Emma thought as the space around them took shape, revealing what appeared to be a large soundstage with various tableaus lighting up one at a time. A scene in a diner, one in a movie theater. One flaring to life after another. But in every one, Sam was always alone—either because Emma was late or she had to leave early.

After a final flash of a scene of Sam sitting alone in his apartment, in front of a table set for two, a pair of candles burned down more than halfway, Corey looked over at Emma, one blond eyebrow arched admonishingly. "You sure made this guy wait around a lot."

Emma bristled, not sure if it was with exasperation or shame. "You're enjoying this, aren't you?"

"Come on. What's not to enjoy? The whole hitting rock bottom is always the best part of the story. Actually—" Corey raised his index finger. "I take that back." He grinned. "The best part is coming up next."

⁂

THE COLORFUL MIST came into focus to reveal the kitchen of her parents' house, dark for an instant, then the flick of a switch sent the spacious room into view. Her father was slipping off his coat while her mother moved to the counter to make them coffee. Based on the length of her mother's graying bob, Emma suspected she was being shown a scene from the past—though not-too-distant a past. Photo holiday cards wallpapered the front of the fridge—Happy New Year 2017!

She cast an expectant look in Corey's direction. What were they doing here?

"Admit it, Phil." Her mother's voice pulled Emma's attention back to the scene. Jo Wallace was scooping grounds into the basket, a small smile growing on her lips. "You like him."

Liked *who?* Emma wondered.

"He seems nice enough," her father said with a shrug, taking a seat at the breakfast bar. "And he has a decent job. Although I'm not sure how much architects make."

Sam. They were talking about Sam. Her heart pounded with pride. Just like her, they'd taken to him from the start.

But as pleasing as it was to know her parents had gushed over Sam within hours of meeting him, she still felt the mounting despair of having to watch yet another scene reminding her of how fantastic he was.

She looked up at Corey. "I know my parents loved Sam. You don't have to—"

"Shh." He pressed his finger to his lips then swung the same finger toward the scene to guide her gaze back. "This isn't about Sam. It's about *you.* Watch."

"He's perfect for her," her mother said, holding the carafe under the tap.

Her father's smile tilted warily. "If he's so perfect then why do you look so worried?"

"Because I'm terrified she's going to push him away just like she did Scott and Ethan—and that boy from college who wore flip-flops in the middle of winter…"

"Michael," her father said. "Although I'm not sure that boy was such a huge loss."

Corey snickered loudly, but Emma continued to frown, still hanging on her mother's earlier comment.

"Did she really think I pushed them away?" she whispered to herself.

"Ouch, right?" Corey said, leaning over. "Your own mother knew you'd blow this."

Emma glared up at him, even as her stomach sank. "I thought you said no talking."

The coffee brewing, her mother came around the breakfast bar and joined her father. "She's always been so fixated on her career."

"There's nothing wrong with that, Jo. I'm proud of her ambition."

"Well, of course. I am too," her mother agreed, her voice too thin with concern to carry a defensive edge. "But why does it have to be one or the other?"

Again, her father could only offer a weak shrug. "She thinks it does."

"Or maybe it's just an excuse to avoid getting her heart broken." Her mother dropped onto the bar's other stool, her shoulders rounding with defeat. "I should have talked to her more. I should have let her know that just because I made the choice I did, she doesn't have to do the same." She sighed. "I think she had it in her head that I was sorry I left my career."

Her father's dark eyes were tender. "And were you?"

In the sudden hush, while her mother deliberated, Emma

wasn't sure she continued to breathe. All her life she'd made assumptions, thinking her father had never cared to ask.

After another moment, her mother smiled serenely. "Never."

Emma felt the prickle of tears, the confirmation dizzying. Through blurry eyes, she watched her father reach over and take her mother's hands where they lay in her lap, squeezing them into his. "Don't be so hard on yourself, Jo. I was there too. I could have done more. Been more generous..."

Her heart swelled with emotion. She could count on one hand the times her father had admitted regret about anything.

Her mother's face softened as she scanned his, and Emma felt the sting of her own regret. She'd been wrong to think her mother had wished for something different for herself.

Emma swallowed hard, but the knot of remorse stuck.

She'd been wrong about a lot of things.

Her father's voice deepened, her mother's hands still in his. "Give it time, Jo. They're just getting to know each other. It's only been a few weeks."

"But the way she looks at him..." Her mother smiled. "A mother knows."

Overcome, Emma charged toward her parents, desperate to connect with them, to tell them she understood clearly now, but as soon as she moved closer, the room began to fade until she was alone again with Corey in a swirl of silvery-white nothingness.

She stared into the blankness, her voice thin with shock. "I told myself I would be different," she said quietly. "That I wouldn't let a guy make me choose my work or him."

And yet, somewhere along the way, she'd done the very thing she'd vowed never to let a man do. Not Sam, but *her*. Sam had never asked her to give up her career—or even asked her to choose.

She'd made that choice for both of them.

Sam was right; so was her mother. Her career had never been the reason her relationships hadn't worked out. *She* was.

Emma lowered her head, regret making her so dizzy she had to close her eyes to stay balanced. "Now I understand why you wanted to end on this scene," she whispered, wiping her eyes dry with the edges of her thumbs.

"Oh no," Corey said. "We're not done yet."

Something in the narrowing of his gaze sent panic rippling through her chest.

Then the world of white began swirling again.

Chapter Eighteen

WHEN THE MIST cleared this time, Emma didn't recognize her surroundings. She and Corey had arrived in a living room decorated for the holiday with a big, twinkling tree and a roaring fire, the fireplace mantel draped in pine boughs and splashes of holly berries. Christmas jazz purred from a speaker set recessed somewhere in the pumpkin-colored wood that covered the walls and vaulted ceiling. Emma even detected the sweet, spicy smell of recently baked gingerbread.

She looked over at Corey. "Where are we?"

Before he could answer, a pretty woman in her thirties with a loose auburn braid stepped into the room, an ornament in her hand.

"Who's that?" Emma asked.

"Beautiful, isn't she?"

Emma frowned—that wasn't an answer, but leave it to Corey to state the obvious. "Yes, she's lovely," she agreed impatiently. "But what does she have to do with—"

Then, through the same doorway, appeared Sam, and Emma's voice froze in her throat.

She stared, unblinking, as he crossed to the woman who stood admiring the tree, the ball ornament still dangling from her hand. When Sam reached up and laid his hands on her shoulders and the woman leaned back into his chest, Emma's breath caught. She wanted to throw herself into the room, to make Sam see her. What she wouldn't give for one more chance to fall into his embrace.

"Her name's Ann," Corey said, looking more like a mooning schoolboy by the second. "And she's apparently *very* available to Sam's needs. At least, that's what it says in my notes."

"But—" Emma's voice came out in a squeak, forcing her to swallow and try again. "But he doesn't know an Ann."

"Apparently they met at Christmas. She came to a party at his parents' house, and they hit it off right away."

"You mean the trip Sam is planning tomorrow?" Emma blinked with confusion, her head spinning as she tried to make sense of this impossible math. "You're saying they're going to meet *this* Christmas?"

Corey shrugged. "Tomorrow, yesterday... It's all the same here."

But was it really? A flutter of relief coursed through Emma when she remembered Sam hadn't yet left for his parents'. She turned to Corey, her voice rising with desperation. "Then this is just a scene of what *could* happen, right?"

"You want to know the best part?" Corey asked, ignoring her question entirely. "Ann's a teacher too."

Alarm scampered up Emma's neck. "What do you mean, a teacher *too*?"

"Oh, yeah, I forgot to show you that part. Adams Elementary asked Sam to join full-time to head up their after-school program, and he agreed."

"They did?"

Finding a good branch, Ann leaned in to settle the metal hanger of the oversized silver ball on the tree, turning it just enough that Emma could read the inscription. *Baby's First Christmas 2022.*

Emma pressed her fingers against her temples, sure she was burning up with fever. *This is just a dream. This isn't real.* But her heart continued to hammer behind her ribs.

A chime broke through the piped-in Christmas music. Corey pulled out his phone, scanned the screen, and announced, "Well, I hate to dream and run, but I'm late for my next appointment." He shoved his phone back into his gym shorts and thrust out his hand. "Hey, Emma, it's been real. Good luck with all of this." He leaned in and whispered, "Between you and me, you're gonna *need* it."

The warmth drained from her face. Around her, the room and all its sounds and smells began to fade. She looked back at Corey, panic sending her pulse racing. "Wait!" she cried. "You didn't answer my question—are these scenes of what *could* happen, or what *will* happen?"

"You should really get some sleep," Corey said, growing as blurry as the room. "You've got a big meeting tomorrow.

Wouldn't want to blow it."

"I don't care about the meeting!" Emma raced after him. "I want to tell Sam I'm sorry. That I've been a selfish, foolish idiot and I'm sorry!"

But the faster she pushed through the swirl of color and sounds, the further Corey moved away, taking any clarity with him.

"Don't leave," Emma cried, having to squint now to see through the murky white. "Please! Come back! *Come back*!"

Chapter Nineteen

"COME BACK!"

Emma bolted upright in bed and blinked into the faint light of dawn that filled her bedroom, gulping air like someone stuck underwater too long.

Scanning her surroundings, relief bloomed. She lunged across her bed for her phone on the nightstand, her fingers trembling as she tapped it to life and saw the date.

December twenty-fourth!

She hadn't missed Christmas Eve!

And even better, it was only 9:10. Surely, Sam hadn't left for his parents' house yet?

Tugging on the first sweater and pair of jeans she found, Emma pulled down a suitcase and designed her plan as she filled it with enough clothes for the weekend. She'd go straight to Sam's apartment and tell him she wanted to make things work—and when they were on their way to his parents' house, she'd call Diane and explain that something had come up so they'd have to reschedule their meeting with Morris. And if there was time, Emma would even ask Sam stop at their favorite bakery and pick up an eggnog cheesecake to bring to his mother.

By the time she was in the car twenty minutes later, Emma was practically floating. Was it the dream's doing? Maybe. Did it matter? Not at all! All she knew was that she couldn't remember a promotion or a job interview or a client meeting that had ever left her feeling this charged and excited—

Until she turned into Sam's driveway and found his car missing.

Then Emma's heart—all of her—*sank.*

But a ping of determination chimed through the disappointment. Not yet ready to surrender, Emma tapped in her phone for Sam's number and formulated her plea while she waited for the call to go through. She'd tell him she was ready to make him, to make *them,* her priority, that she'd been wrong about so many things—

"The subscriber you are trying to reach is out of range…"

Shoot! Emma hung up, ripples of dread flaring up her spine—she should have expected this. Cell service in the mountains near where Sam's parents lived was terrible—that was, in fact, one of the excuses Emma had historically used to get out of visiting his parents, claiming she couldn't risk being out of reach of her team at work. Now her cheeks flared with shame at the reminder. Why had she fought his devotion so hard?

When her phone hummed in her hands, she sucked in a startled gasp, hope tearing through her, until she saw the name on the screen.

She pulled in a steeling breath. "Hi, Diane."

"I caught you. They were out of gingerbread lattes at my coffee shop, so I need you to pick me up one on your way in for the meeting. Oh, and get me an egg-white breakfast sandwich too. I gorged on a mini red velvet cupcake last night, and my blood pressure is through the *roof...*"

Emma closed her door and collapsed against her seat, letting Diane's rambling fade into white noise.

"Emma? Emma, are you there?"

Snapped back, she sat up, forcing an enthusiasm to her voice. "Gingerbread latte, egg-white breakfast sandwich. Got it."

But as soon as Diane disconnected their call, Emma tossed her phone onto the passenger seat, grabbed the steering wheel, and let her forehead fall against her knuckles, feeling the prickle of tears. Even as she fought the urge to cry, she admonished herself for her self-pity. What she should really be feeling was relief, right? What if she'd actually called Diane to cancel on her way to Sam's? Then she'd truly have nothing—no Sam *and* no job.

Emma sat up, a fierce wave of resolve sending her shoulders rolling back—then a flutter of anger tore up her stiffened spine.

So much for second chances. So much for the power of dreams! What had been the point of putting her through all those visits with her ex-boyfriends if she wasn't going to get a chance to do the right thing?

She swiped at her eyes, drying the spilled tears that had refused to be swallowed back anymore.

Fine, then. It had all been one big joke her subconscious had apparently played on herself—ha, ha.

Not sure who she was more furious with—herself, her boss, the universe, or all three—Emma yanked her car into reverse and hit the gas, only to look up and suck in a startled gasp when she saw a white SUV turning in behind her. She slammed on the brakes. Rushing out, she was sure she recognized the woman who leaped out of the driver's side with a worried expression that Emma suspected mirrored her own. A little boy, also vaguely familiar, poked his head up from the back seat to watch the scene.

"I'm so sorry!" the dark-haired woman said, coming around to meet Emma.

"*I'm* sorry," Emma insisted. "I must have scared the daylights out of you."

"It's Emma, right? We met at the school the other day. I'm Gail, and that's my son, Eli." The woman pointed to the SUV, and the little boy ducked back down behind the seat.

"Of course," Emma said, recognition dawning—and with it, a flutter of self-reproach. The woman Sam had trusted to help him see the delivery through in his absence.

Gail's smile remained intact, but her eyes flashed as they flicked anxiously toward Sam's front door. "Is Sam here?"

"I'm afraid not," Emma said, unable to mask the disappointment in her voice this time.

"Oh no…" Defeat washed across the woman's face. "I've been trying to get him on his cell, but I can't get the call to go through."

Emma smiled sadly. "That makes two of us. He's always out of range in the mountains."

"Oh, this is a disaster." Gail threw up her hands and sighed. "The delivery van was on its way to the retirement home and someone rear-ended it. All the cookie baskets were ruined."

"What?" Emma felt the heat of dread crawl up her cheeks—she knew how much work had gone into those baskets. Sam would be beside himself! "How bad was the damage?"

"The baskets are salvageable," Gail said, "but all the cookies are broken. I'd gladly offer up my kitchen to remake them, but we've got my husband's entire family staying with us for the holiday and there's just no way." Gail pushed out a defeated sigh and took a step back, her lips lifted in a brave but far from confident smile. "I'll just keep trying to reach Sam and hope he can think of something," she said as she pulled open the driver's door. "Sorry to have bothered you. Merry Christmas!"

As Emma watched Gail climb back into the driver's seat and turn the engine back on, she caught a glimpse of Eli's worried face popping up behind the seat, the gravity of the situation clear—even if Gail *could* reach Sam once he got to his folks, it would still be too late to have him turn around and come back to try and fix this.

They had to act now.

Emma had to act now.

Even if it meant missing the most important meeting of her career.

"Wait!" Emma darted forward, waving for Gail to stay. Eli's mom rolled down her window when Emma arrived at the door. "We can use my kitchen to remake them."

Gail's eyes widened with hope. "Are you sure?"

Oh, Emma was sure, all right—sure that if she agreed to this and canceled on Diane and Morris Johnson, she'd be axed from the team. Maybe even the whole firm.

But she was sure of something else too, something bigger than any rebranding for Johnson Cookware.

For the first time in possibly her whole life, Emma was sure that doing this for Sam, for Eli, and for all the kids at Adams Elementary, was what she was meant to do. Maybe she hadn't been sent those dreams to save her relationship with Sam—maybe she had been sent them to save *herself.*

Her lips rose in a confident smile as she turned back to Gail. "Absolutely sure."

Chapter Twenty

*S*IXTY DOZEN COOKIES.

Until they arrived at Emma's apartment and opened the trunk of Gail's SUV to reveal the sea of bags of baking supplies, Emma hadn't quite wrapped her head around the work they had ahead of them to repair the lost baskets. But somehow Emma felt uniquely fortified. After all, making sixty dozen cookies couldn't be any harder than calling her boss to tell her that she wouldn't be able to make the meeting of her career—and Emma had already done that.

The call to Diane—made while Gail had rushed Eli to the restroom at the market—had gone about as badly as Emma had expected. In the span of four minutes, Diane had spun from rage to begging then back to rage again, capping off her manic performance with a single declaration. Emma was not only off the account, she was out of a job at Zenith. Even as she'd hung up, Emma suspected the reality of her firing would eventually hit her like the Grinch's filled sleigh, but for the time being, all she could have thought about was getting back to her apartment and rescuing Kids Who Cook.

"I apologize for the mess," Emma said as she led Gail and

Eli inside her townhouse, the heat of embarrassment warming her cheeks to find the piles of dishes and strewn clothes she'd so blissfully abandoned a few hours earlier, when she'd been sure she had time to catch Sam before he left town.

Gail just smiled as she set down a stack of cookie sheets. "Oh please—you haven't seen *mess* until you have six nieces and nephews sleeping in your living room for a week."

⁂

JOBS WERE ALLOCATED quickly. Eli would clean out the baskets of cookie crumbs and reorganize the handmade cards from the students, while Emma and Gail would start on the dough. An hour into their efforts, the cooling racks already began to boast several batches of beautifully golden cookies.

Then Gail broke the bad news. Each cookie had to be monogrammed.

"Every single one?" Emma blinked at her.

Gail nodded with a sheepish smile. "I'm afraid so—that's everyone's favorite part." She plucked out her phone and scrolled through her emails. "Luckily, I still have the list of all the residents somewhere in my old… here it is!"

When Gail handed Emma the filled piping bag a few moments later, Emma stared at it then up at Gail. "You want *me* to write the names?"

"Sam said you were an artist."

"I design graphics on a computer," Emma said warily.

"It's not exactly the same."

"Well, I majored in marine biology, so between the two of us, you're *definitely* more suited to the job."

Emma grinned. "Good point," she said, taking the piping bag and settling in to work. Her first few attempts were legible, if far from pretty, but after a few more, Emma found her rhythm—and soon she and Gail were in step, a collection of frosted cookies growing steadily at the end of the counter. At his mother's request, Eli had found a holiday music station to stream on her phone, and the warm tone of Nat King Cole's "The Christmas Song" sailed through the kitchen. Emma had to admit the festive music helped their pace—then she had to smile, remembering how she'd groused over Denise's constant playing of Christmas carols at the office.

What a difference a few days could make.

"He seems like a really great guy." Gail's comment drew Emma back from her wandering thoughts. She looked over to find Eli's mom's brown eyes pooling with warmth. "Sam," the woman clarified, taking Emma's finished cookie and adding it to the pile.

"He is," she said softly. "The best." A knot of regret clumped in her throat, and Emma tried to swallow it down as she glanced over at Gail's master list, wanting to steer them back to safer subjects. "Next name?"

"Edward," Gail said, then let a beat pass before resuming their earlier subject. Emma could hear the gentle edge of curiosity in the woman's voice. "I didn't want to pry earlier, but I thought Sam said you and he were going to his parents' for the holiday?"

"We were. Well. *He* still is. Just not with me."

Gail nodded, a small but sad smile lifting her lips as she sighed. "You think it must be so easy making a relationship work, you know? We grow up watching movies, reading books, and it looks so simple. Effortless, right? That if you have love and passion, you don't need to worry."

Now it was Emma's turn to inquire. "It's not my business, but are you and Eli's dad…"

"Still together?" Gail's dark eyes were tender and without a trace of offense at Emma's question. "We're still married, yes. But *together*? Well. That's another question. He's on the road a lot. When we had Eli, we agreed to take turns. I was working full-time and didn't want to give up my career."

"So did you?"

"I ended up choosing to be part-time, but I'm still not always decided. Some days I want to stop working entirely, and other days I don't." Her smile turned wistful. "I always thought I'd know for sure, that it would be clear. I waited for so long, thinking there would be some magical sign that it was the right time to do everything. Get married, start a family."

Emma set down the piping bag. "Was there?" she asked carefully. "A right time, I mean?"

"If there was, I must have missed seeing it." Gail's gaze

shifted suddenly to where Eli sat at Emma's breakfast table, the boy deep in concentration as he tied ribbons around the cookie stacks they'd taken turns nestling in plastic wrap. "All I know is that life works out the way it's supposed to. Despite all our plans and our deadlines."

Deadlines don't take holidays...

Again the memory of her frequent mantra made Emma's skin flush with shame. But this time, she felt the flare of pride too. Despite everything her commitment to her work had possibly cost her, that same dedication would repair this unfortunate accident and get these cookie baskets delivered as promised.

"You realize when he sees how you've stepped in and made this happen, Sam will want you back, don't you?" Gail said.

Hope swelled, but the weight of regret tamped it down. Emma felt the prickle of tears well behind her eyes.

She bit her lip to stem them, but her voice cracked with defeat. "I'm worried I pushed him too far this time."

Gail laid her hand on Emma's as it held the piping bag. "Don't be so hard on yourself. He's obviously crazy about you."

How Emma wanted to believe she still had a chance. But doubt prevailed. "What you said before about timing..." She glanced over at Gail. "I suppose I keep waiting to know for sure."

"You won't. You *don't*. That's the trap, I think. Imagining you're ever one hundred percent sure." She smiled. "When the truth is you just have to have faith and jump in."

"Mommy, I'm out of ribbon!" Eli's panicked cry from the other side of the kitchen was a welcomed interruption. Emma's eyes starting to fill, she blinked hard to stop the spill of tears and set out to finish decorating the last of the cookies while Gail hurried to Eli's side.

❧

AN HOUR LATER, twenty-four freshly filled baskets covered every surface in Emma's kitchen—and it was a beautiful sight.

Looking out onto the spread of their efforts, Emma felt a swell of pride. Just four hours earlier, they'd been facing complete failure. And now there was a fairly good chance that no one would ever know of the hiccup that had nearly derailed the program.

"All these dishes," Gail said with a mournful sigh as she turned to face the stacks of bowls and utensils that towered in Emma's sink.

"Just leave them," Emma said, already reaching for her coat. So behind schedule, she didn't even have time to change out of her frosting and flour-splattered shirt, let alone clean her kitchen. "I'll take care of it when I get back."

"Get back?" Gail blinked at her. "You want to help with the delivery?"

"Of course," Emma said, startled at the woman's bemused stare.

"But..." Gail's brow continued to wrinkle with worry. "But you've already given up your whole Christmas Eve day. Surely you must have other plans?"

"None that more important than this," Emma said cheerfully, filling her arms with several baskets and moving for the door.

Chapter Twenty-One

THE ENTRANCE TO Sunshine Village Retirement Home was true to its name, Emma thought as she stepped through the sliding glass doors into a large room, bathed in sunlight and sparkling with holiday decor. The walls were painted in warm, soft shades of peach and coral, and grass rugs underfoot gave the space a breezy, beachy feeling. And weren't retirement homes supposed to smell of mothballs and disinfectant spray? Not here. The smell of gingerbread floated, thick and warm, and where Emma would have expected to hear the syrupy strings of Muzak piped in the background, the bright, cheery sounds of big band music played instead.

"Help you, dear?" a plump woman with a cloud of frizzy blond hair called to Emma from the reception counter, no doubt having seen Emma gaping helplessly in the foyer.

Emma rushed across the room, pleased to find several more smiling faces on the other side of the desk when she arrived. "We're from Kids Who Cook. I'm sorry we're behind schedule. We had a little bit of a hiccup getting everything here but—"

"You made it!"

Before Emma could finish, the entire staff behind the desk rushed from their chairs.

"Oh, we were so worried," a woman with bright pink hair and blinking Christmas ball earrings said.

Another in a crooked Santa hat concurred. "When we didn't see the van all morning, we were so nervous something had happened!"

The thin woman leaned over the counter and announced, "Everyone! The cookies are here! Mary," she said, turning to the woman with pink hair. "Call Dale to help bring the baskets in, will you?"

Within seconds, the hushed room grew loud with excited voices and the shuffling of chairs as residents rose from their seats and moved toward the entryway where Gail and Eli appeared.

Emma waved them over. "These are the real Santa's elves," she said, stepping back to make the introductions. As expected, the crowd gathered quickly around Eli, who wasn't shy about dazzling the grandparent set with his harrowing tale of rescue.

"And you remade all these cookies by yourself?" one resident with a wispy white bun asked him.

"That's right—and we used her kitchen," Eli announced proudly, hooking his thumb in Emma's direction before he leaned closer to the woman and lowered his voice to add, "It was already *really* messy so I don't think she minded too much."

Gail, looking mortified, offered Emma an apologetic glance—but Emma just smiled.

"First, a picture," a staff member exclaimed, holding up her cell phone. "I want to get a shot for the Facebook page!"

"Me too!" came another cry. "A video! I'm going to put it up on the Sunshine Village newsfeed."

So, while the baskets were wheeled in, Emma, Gail, and Eli posed for pictures and offered quick interviews. Emma couldn't believe the reception. She'd known the Christmas Cookie Basket Brigade had been well-received when Sam had started it two years ago, but looking around now at the elated faces of the staff and the residents, she'd never realized it meant so much, and her heart ached with longing. Sam should have been here. Their breakup was only a few hours old, and already Emma missed him as if he'd been gone for months.

"You can't know how much the residents look forward to this." The woman who had first welcomed Emma over to the reception desk came beside her now. "Please say you'll stay to see the residents receive their baskets?"

Emma glanced at Gail, who offered her an absolving smile. "Don't feel you have to stay," the woman said. "You've already done so much."

But she hadn't. Compared to all that Sam had done, all that the rest of them did every day, Emma hadn't even *begun* to do her part—this season, or *any* season.

But starting today, that was going to change.

Besides. If she couldn't be in Sam's arms right now, then Emma couldn't think of anywhere she'd rather be.

"I'd love to," she said.

Chapter Twenty-Two

IF EMMA THOUGHT their efforts had been appreciated *before* the baskets were handed out, seeing the looks on the residents' faces when they read the handcrafted Christmas cards from the students proved even more heartwarming. She couldn't know if it was the sweet, buttery smells of sugar cookies and hot mulled cider, the flames that crackled in the large stone fireplace, or the carols that rang out over the loudspeakers, but whatever the source, Emma had never felt the spirit of Christmas more than she did at that moment.

So why did pangs of loneliness continue to prickle her skin like gooseflesh?

Looking around for Gail and Eli, Emma saw mother and son making their way toward the exit, a few fans still keeping them company as they walked. Thinking it was likely time for her to break the spell of this magic day too, Emma made her goodbyes, stopping by the reception center on her way out to wish the staff a Merry Christmas.

Almost at the sliding front doors, Emma spotted a white-haired woman in a silver-sequin-studded cardigan struggling to hold a pair of potted poinsettias while she waited for the elevator.

Fearing the woman might lose one or both plants, Emma hurried to help. "Let me take one for you," she said, arriving just in time to relieve the woman of one pot and set it down on a nearby bench.

"Bless you, dear," the elderly woman said, offering Emma a warm smile that made her blue eyes sparkle like freshly fallen snow. "You're quite the miracle lady, aren't you? Two rescues in one day."

Emma smiled bashfully. "I wouldn't go *that* far…"

"Don't be so sure." The older woman's smile was as bright as her eyes. "You've made a lot of people very happy, Miss…"

"Emma. Emma Wallace."

"It's nice to meet you, Emma Wallace," the older woman said. "I'm Beatrice Snow. I've lived here at Sunshine Village for almost ten years now."

Beatrice. Emma's thoughts spun back to her morning spent carefully writing all those names in frosting. Curious. She didn't recall decorating a cookie for someone named Beatrice…

"We'll wait for you out front, Emma," Gail said as she and Eli walked past for the front doors.

Emma nodded and turned back to Beatrice. "Will you be able to get those upstairs?" she asked, pointing to the poinsettias.

"I'll just make two trips. Don't worry about me." The older woman hitched her chin in the direction of the exit. "I don't want you to keep your friends waiting."

"It was lovely to meet you," Emma said, starting for the doors. "And Merry Christmas."

"Merry Christmas to you too. Oh, and dear?"

Emma turned back to find Beatrice wearing a warm smile. "Have faith."

Emma blinked at her, confused. "Excuse me?"

The elevator door opened and Beatrice stepped halfway in, holding the door back as she said, "The dreams work in mysterious ways, but they work. I should know. I nearly let Robert slip away once. And next year will be our seventieth anniversary."

Emma was sure her face had turned the color of poinsettia petals as she watched Beatrice step fully into the elevator and the doors closed behind her.

Turning for the exit, she slowed when she saw the man standing with Gail and Eli at the front of their SUV, and her breath caught in her throat.

Sam.

Chapter Twenty-Three

STEPPING OUT INTO the falling snow, all Emma could hear was the racing of her pulse in her ears. Halfway across the parking lot, she slowed her steps, filled with a sudden fear that Sam might not have wanted her to know he had come, that now that she'd seen him he might leave without letting her reach him, but when his gaze turned to meet hers, only tenderness and affection burned there.

Emma felt sure her heart would leap right out of her chest. "Sam," she whispered as she hastened her pace across the snow-dusted pavement, seeing he was now doing the same.

But before he could reach her, Eli dashed around him. "Emma!" The boy's puffy arms were outstretched as he raced toward her, Gail's phone held high. "Emma, look! We're all over everywhere!"

Confused, Emma took the phone from Eli's hand and stared down at the screen, seeing the video of her and Gail and Eli arriving with the cookie baskets.

"See, Emma, see?" Eli exclaimed, breathless from his sprint—and his excitement. "Mommy says we're *vinyl*."

Only a few steps behind her son, Gail smothered a laugh into her glove. "He means *viral*."

"It's all over the internet, Em," Sam said as he arrived beside her. "Someone tagged Kids Who Cook about this story of Santa's miracle elves who saved the day, and it just blew up."

Stunned, Emma blinked at the screen for several more seconds before handing the phone back to Gail. "I had no idea."

"We even have our own hashtag," Gail said. "#christmas-cookierescuers. Not bad, huh?"

"And Chef Sam, I tied all the ribbons myself!" Eli announced proudly.

Sam reached down to ruffle the snow off Eli's flurry-dusted hat. "I think that calls for a promotion, *Chef* Eli."

The boy's eyes grew huge. "*Really?*"

"Really."

"Mommy, did you hear that?" Eli spun toward Gail. "Chef Sam called *me* chef!"

Gail shot Sam an appreciative smile as she took Eli's hand, her eyes flashing with quiet understanding when she looked over at Emma, then at Sam. "We should really be going," she said, already helping Eli into the backseat.

"Gail," Sam said, "how can I thank you for all this?"

"Emma's the hero here," Gail said, then winked in Emma's direction before adding, "but if you wash all those dishes she got left with, I think we'll be square."

Sam smiled. "Done," he said, already turning his gaze back to find Emma's.

Stepping back, they waved Gail's SUV off into the thickening curtain of flurries. Alone at last, they looked at one another, the brisk, snowy air charged with longing. Emma wanted to rush into Sam's arms, to throw her arms around his neck and hold on forever, but she didn't yet dare. Her heart hammered, pounding in her ears. Could he hear it in the flurried hush too?

His eyes searched hers. "I don't know what to say."

She shook her head, sending snowflakes falling around her. Her hands tingled to touch him. "I'm the one who should be saying something. Starting with I'm sorry."

"Em…"

"No, Sam, you were right. I've been using my career to keep us from getting closer, because I know in my heart you're the one and I'm just so scared."

"You don't think I'm scared too?" When his strained features broke into a warm smile, the heat of it spread across her face like a fever. She exhaled a breath of equal parts joy and relief. "Wait." Panic flickered suddenly across his face. "Your meeting this morning—the account… Em, don't tell me you missed the meeting to save my program."

She smiled and reached up to brush off the fine layer of flurries that had settled above his temple. "Or maybe I was saving us."

When she lowered her gloved hand, Sam took it. "Emma, this wasn't about you giving up your job. I never asked you to do that."

"I know you didn't." Her heart still pounding, another fear sparked, flaring hot across her chilled cheeks. "Sam, I want you to know I didn't mean for this to be some promotional stunt. I didn't mean for this to be about *me*."

He tipped her face up to his and answered her with a long, hard kiss, pressing his mouth over hers until she felt the worried line of her lips soften. Whatever breath she'd been holding sailed free, mingling with his then coiling like smoke between their faces when he released her.

"You believe me, don't you?" she pressed, mining his eyes for proof.

"Of course, I know you didn't mean that."

She reared up and kissed him, pulling in a deep whiff of his spicy scent before lowering herself back down. "And another thing," she said, keeping her arms locked around his neck just in case he doubted her conviction. "I want you to know, if you want to take the job at the school, I fully support you."

He blinked down at her.

"You don't believe me?"

"No, it's not that. It's just..." Sam was suddenly pale— now who looked like they'd seen ghosts? "How did you know they offered me a position? The school board only called me this morning."

Emma shrugged helplessly. "I guess I just figured after

seeing how much they loved you there, that it was only a matter of time before they offered you a job."

But Sam's gaze remained firm on hers, his brow still bent with suspicion. "You said *the* job, Em—not *a* job." The chime of her phone hummed from inside her coat, rescuing her, but when she didn't move to answer, Sam said, "Don't you even want to see who it is?"

"I'm sure it's nothing," Emma said, reaching in to silence the ring. But when her gaze glimpsed the caller ID, she froze. She looked up at Sam. "It's Morris Johnson," she whispered. "He's the CEO of Johnson Cookware."

Sam nodded to the phone still chiming in her hand. "Then you should take it," he said firmly. And this time, there was no exasperation, no frustration, in his voice—only absolute encouragement.

She swallowed hard and clicked to connect. "Hi, this is Emma."

"Emma, Morris Johnson here."

"Hello, Mr. Johnson." She pressed her hand against her racing heart, suddenly wishing she'd let the call go to voicemail.

"Why didn't you tell me you already had plans today?"

"Excuse me?" Emma glanced up at Sam as if seeking explanation, but he just stared down at her.

"Emma, don't be modest. I saw you all over Twitter. Well, *someone* in the company who enjoys all this internet foolishness that passes for technological advancement saw you—but the point is, I'm impressed."

Her gaze snapped up to Sam's. "You saw me on *Twitter*?"

"That's right," Morris continued. "Emma, Johnson Cookware is about the spirit of giving back—and what you did for this organization is not only on brand, but on message. You didn't just design a campaign for how food can bring people together—you've proven that you *live* it. And I can't think of a better person to rebrand our company."

Emma took Sam's hand and squeezed. "Are you saying..." She paused, almost not daring to let the possibility out. "Are you saying you want me on the account?"

"Not just on the account. I want you *leading* it."

Butterflies of alarm fluttered. As much as she didn't want to break the spell of this incredible offer, she had to be clear with him. "Mr. Johnson, you do realize I'm no longer at Zenith, don't you? I understand if that's a problem—"

"Are you kidding? It's a bonus! Between you and me, dealing with Diane was causing my hair to fall out—and considering how much I went through to put it back on my head, I'm more than happy to lose her in the deal."

Emma bit back a chuckle, her excitement swelling again.

"And another thing," Morris said, "we're so crazy about this organization of yours, we'd like to be Kids Who Cook's official sponsor. How does all this sound?"

Still gripping Sam's hand, Emma closed her eyes, willing her heart to slow its pounding long enough for her to speak.

"This all sounds wonderful."

"Good. We'll draw up all the paperwork and make it official after the holidays. Oh, and Emma?"

She let her eyes open. "Yes?"

"Merry Christmas."

"Merry Christmas, Mr. Johnson," she said, not sure if it was all of her, or just her fingers, that trembled as she hung up the call and slid her phone back into her pocket.

"Well?" Sam pulled her close, scanning her eyes quizzically. "What did he say?"

"He said—" Emma stopped, feeling a forgotten bulk in her pocket, and looked up at him. "Are you hungry?"

"Am I hungry?" He looked at her blankly. "Em, you're killing me here. What did he say? And what did you mean, you're no longer with Zenith?"

She just kept smiling up at him. "Are you?"

"Well, yeah, I'm starving, but—"

"Good." She pulled out the sandwich bag she'd been carrying for the past two hours and carefully extracted the two cookies she'd kept safe inside. "We had a little leftover dough," she explained as she held them up, two sides of one cookie heart. "They fit together, see?"

Sam took a cookie, his eyes pooling with affection as he slid it against her half and held it there. "What do you know? It's a perfect match."

Tears welled, but these were the good kind. And this time, she wasn't afraid to let them spill. "We always have been, Sam," she whispered. "I was just too stuck to see it."

He grinned. "If I eat this, do you promise to tell me what's going on?"

"Only if you promise we can make more."

His eyes shimmered with heat. "I promise we'll be making more of a lot of things, Emma Wallace," he whispered as he pulled her into his arms and lowered his lips over hers. "For a long, long time."

The End

A yummy recipe fit for any season! (And while you don't need to make sixty dozen of these, like our heroine did for Kids Who Cook, no one will judge if you do!)

Sugar Cookies

Makes 2 dozen

2 ½ cups flour

½ teaspoon baking soda

½ teaspoon salt

¼ teaspoon cinnamon

1 cup (2 sticks) unsalted butter, softened

½ cup granulated sugar

1 tsp lemon extract (you can substitute vanilla if you don't have lemon)

1 egg

1. Mix flour, baking soda, salt and cinnamon together. Set aside.

2. Beat butter and sugar until blended in a large bowl.

3. Beat in egg and lemon.

4. Stir in flour mixture until just blended.

5. Split dough in half. Wrap two halves in plastic wrap, or waxed paper, and refrigerate for at least an hour.

6. When you're ready to bake your cookies, preheat oven to 350 degrees F.

7. Using a rolling pin, roll out dough on a lightly floured surface and cut with cookie cutters of your choice.

8. Lay out on ungreased cookie sheet and bake for 10 minutes, until bottoms are a very light brown.

9. Let cool fully before decorating with icing—or serve as is!

If you enjoyed this book, please leave a review at your favorite online retailer! Even if it's just a sentence or two it makes all the difference.

Thanks for reading *Boyfriends of Christmas Past* by Edie Grace!

Discover your next romance at TulePublishing.com.

TULE
PUBLISHING

If you enjoyed *Boyfriends of Christmas Past*, you'll love these other Tule Christmas books!

Rescued by Christmas
by Erika Marks

Jingle Bells and Wedding Vows
by Barbara Dunlop

A Christmas Romance
by Nancy Holland

Christmas Comes to Snowfall
by Erika Marks

The Christmas Contest
by Scarlet Wilson

About the Author

Hooked on happy-endings from her first episode of *The Love Boat* at seven, Edie Grace lives in Maryland where she writes romantic fiction under the constant supervision of a big-boned cat, and who has never met a bottle of wine she couldn't find something nice to say about. (Edie, that is. Not the cat.)

Follow her on Twitter @EdieGraceBooks

Thank you for reading

Boyfriends of Christmas Past

If you enjoyed this book, you can find more from all our great authors at TulePublishing.com, or from your favorite online retailer.

TULE
PUBLISHING

Made in United States
North Haven, CT
28 November 2021

11669815R00095